DENNY CRADOCK, proceeding under easy steam across the Indian Ocean, swung majestically round the edge of a small coppice and brought up all standing, with much signalling and counter-signalling to the engine-room, beside the pier at Aden (a split rail fence with a gate in it).

Denny was the only son of his mother, and she was a widow. Consequently, having no brother to play with, he was accustomed to invent games which a man can play by himself. It is true he possessed two sisters, Joan and Molly; but he would have shrunk with horror from the idea of inviting either to participate in his present exercises. Joan would have waxed extremely humorous over the idea of a boy of nearly fourteen solemnly pretending to be a P. & O. liner proceeding from Bombay to London; while Molly, though thrilled by the honour of the invitation and anxious to co-operate, would have been quite incapable of appreciating the technical niceties of the game.

7

Denny was an imaginative boy, a sensitive boy, and, above all, a self-conscious boy. Self-conscious people are apt to be secretive, and unless they are absolutely certain that you are a kindred spirit, they keep themselves to themselves and guard their own dreams. If you endeavour to penetrate within the sanctuary of their minds, even with the kindliest of intentions, they will sometimes go so far as to lie to you to put you off the scent. If asked to explain, for instance, why he was now standing motionless beside a split rail fence gazing into vacuity and making a noise like a muted trombone, Denny might—I say he might—have explained to his mother, who always understood, that he was coaling, and that the captain had ordered the ship's band to play. But he most certainly would not have risked imparting such a confidence to an inquisitive and sardonically inclined young sister of twelve. He would have said that he was watching a bird's nest—or, more simply, have recommended her to go home and burst.

Presently, having warped himself from Aden Pier with a lateral shuffle, Denny passed through the gate in the fence (the Straits of Bab-el-Mandeb) and steamed up the Red Sea towards the Isthmus of Suez.

His course for the next few hundred miles

being now set, he summoned a meeting of officers to the captain's cabin and discussed within himself certain matters which promised shortly to send the good ship *Denis Cradock* sailing upon unknown and uncharted seas. For Denny had won a scholarship at Eaglescliffe, and was to depart for that ancient seminary of sound learning almost immediately. The last two days had been rather thrilling. When we are old, and the sheer adventure of leaving port and heading for the horizon has lost its glamour, we set out for China or Peru with as little concern or ceremony as a man walks down the street to buy a stamp at the post office. But the first breaking of home ties is a most solemn business. Denny had been bidding a systematic good-bye to the parish of Ripleigh for nearly a week. To-day matters were approaching the grand climax. He was on his way to a ceremonial tea-party of farewell at " Middlefield," the most considerable house in the district, the home—in fact, one might almost go so far as to call it the seat—of the Bagbys.

The Bagby *ménage* consisted of Mr. Bagby, a kind-hearted, fussy, utterly futile person of about fifty-five, and his lady wife, a few years younger, chiefly remarkable for a hypochrondriacal temperament and a yearning

A*

affection for an entirely unresponsive son and daughter. Mr. and Mrs. Bagby had married comparatively late in life—so late, indeed, that memories of their own childhood had long faded from their minds, with the result that they experienced some difficulty in understanding their offspring, or, indeed, the heart of youth at all. They assumed, for instance, that since their son Lionel—addressed by his doting mother as Little Leo, and referred to by the Cradock family among themselves as Lionel the Terrible—was roughly of an age with Denny Cradock and a near neighbour, that the two boys must as a matter of course be " great chums."

" Denny Cradock will not have your position later in life, darling," Mrs. Bagby once explained to her son. " His mother is only moderately well off, and she has three children to educate ; but one should never allow social distinctions to influence one in one's selection of one's friends, should one ? So you would like to invite Denny over to tea this afternoon, and have a romp with him in the plantations afterwards, wouldn't you ? "

" No," replied Little Leo.

However, chums the boys were declared to be, despite Little Leo's passionate asseverations to the contrary. He was a youth of high spirit, and the fact that his parents had decided upon one course of action was all that was required, as a rule, to send him automatically and victoriously in the opposite direction. Not that he disliked Denny. Secretly, he rather admired him—his muscle, his fleetness of foot, and his obvious abhorrence of such persons as himself—but a principle was at stake, and Lionel the Terrible was a true son of John Bull.

Denny, on his part, regarded his official chum as a milksop and an oaf. Otherwise he harboured no ill-feeling towards him whatever.

Having threaded the Suez Canal, a tortuous pathway between two clumps of laurel, Denny emerged into the Mediterranean—a broad pasture meadow with a stile in the far corner.

Seated on the stile, in the company of an upright gentleman just past middle age, was a little girl in a blue linen frock—a rather misleading little girl, with dreamy eyes and an appealing mouth and an aureole of bright golden hair. She looked like a cherub recently promoted to legs. In reality she was something entirely different—Denny's sister Joan.

" Here comes old Johnny Head-in-Air, Uncle Tony," she announced as Denny approached. " I bet you he's pretending to be something, and hasn't seen us."

" Pretending to be something ? "

" Yes. He's quite mad. He always thinks he's a train, or a man-of-war, or an aeroplane. You see—he'll stop and blow off steam, or loop the loop, or something, in a minute."

Uncle Tony chuckled.

" You're not imaginative, Joan," he suggested.

" I've got some sense, if that's what you mean," replied the young lady composedly. She inserted two slim fingers into her angelic mouth and emitted an ear-splitting whistle. " Hallo, star-gazer ! " she shouted. " What are you to-day ? Wake up ! "

Denny, deep in thought, suddenly called back to the realities of this world and the existence of unfeeling young sisters, came to himself with a start, blushed violently, and then tackled the situation with commendable and brotherly promptitude. He simply made a rush, tipped his sister over backwards into a conveniently adjacent heap of newly-mown grass, and took her seat upon the stile.

" That will be all from you," he announced ; then turned to his uncle and continued, as one man to another : " Hallo, Uncle Tony ! I hope this kid hasn't been bothering you."

" Not at all," replied Uncle Tony. " Joan is a most stimulating companion. Where are you off to this fine afternoon ? "

" Tea at Middlefield," replied Denny.

"Don't blush," urged Joan, resuming her perch and brushing wisps of grass from her short skirt. Naturally Denny blushed at once.

"Is there romance connected with Middle-field?" inquired Uncle Tony.

"I've got to go and have tea with that little skunk Leo Bagby," explained Denny.

"Lionel the Terrible," observed Joan. "He is hated by all."

"He doesn't sound very romantic," said Uncle Tony.

"A lady," announced Joan with a seraphic smile, "will also be present at the tea-party."

"Dry up, Joan!" said Denny uneasily. He was suspected, not entirely without reason, of a youthful tenderness for Little Leo's sister Gwen, a year or two his senior.

"He's blushing again. Isn't he awful, Uncle Tony?" demanded Joan compassionately.

"Joan, you must learn to respect masculine reserve. It is a thing which young females know nothing about. Denny and I are in alliance against you on that point."

"All right," replied Joan affably. "I won't rag him any more, as he's going away so soon. How long are you going to stay at your party, Denny?"

"About an hour, I suppose, unless Lionel the Terrible starts a fight with his father, or the governess, or anybody; then I may get out sooner."

"Well, don't be long. Uncle Tony has promised to tell us some more stories about the I.C.S."

"What's that?"

"The Indian Civil Service," said Joan carelessly. "Didn't you know?"

She had made an entire and bloodless conquest of her grand-uncle since his arrival from India a week ago, and was herself by this time a seasoned Anglo-Indian. At schoolroom meals she made a point of asking the respectfully mystified Molly to pass the *pani* or the *dudh*, and was full of mysterious and important references to such tremendous things as memsahibs, and tiffin, and *chota hazir*.

"Don't show off," said Denny coldly. He turned to his god-father. "When are you going to begin, Uncle Tony?"

"After tea, I believe."

"Wait till I come home, will you?"

"Certainly. Is that agreeable to you, Joan?"

Joan affected to consider.

"If you don't turn up by six," she announced presently, "we'll know that you're washing Gwen's dog for her, the same as last time, and we won't wait. Come on, Uncle Tony! Mother will be expecting you."

She slid off the fence and offered a braced shoulder.

" Lean on me," she said, " and I'll help you down."

" I am not yet entirely decrepit, Joan," replied Uncle Tony gravely ; " but I appreciate the kind thought."

" Oh, that's all right," said Joan. " So long, Denny ! Be good, my child, and give my love to dear little Gwenny."

With this parting shot Miss Joan began to pilot her elderly relative back across the field in the direction of Abbot's Mill, while a some-what ruffled P. & O. liner resumed its voyage up the English Channel.

FIVE minutes later, Denny, emerging from Middlefield shrubberies, found himself close to the house. The late September sun was beginning to slant through the beech trees on the lawn, dappling the ground beneath, and all was drowsy peace.

Denny, who was always a little shy of the Middlefield butler, avoided the front door and cut across the lawn towards the school-room. His course took him past the library. The French windows stood wide open, and within Denny was conscious of the form of a rather dapper little gentleman in tweeds, crouching in a constrained attitude over something in the middle of the room. It was Mr. Bagby. Hearing Denny's step on the gravel, Mr. Bagby cried out, without moving :

" Is that you, Leo ? Come in here, sir, at once."

" It's me, Mr. Bagby," replied Denny, pausing outside and politely removing his cap.

" Oh ! " he said. " Come and give me a hand,

will you, like a good chap ? That young whelp has been at it again."

Realising without difficulty that Mr. Bagby was referring to his only son, Denny entered the library by the open window. Mr. Bagby, holding a large piece of pink blotting paper in his hand, was executing a species of stealthy toe-dance round an inlaid lacquer table. In the centre of the table, serene and glistening, lay a large pool of ink ; beside it a common penny ink-bottle, overturned.

" Dirty little devil ! " observed Mr. Bagby earnestly, still referring, it seemed, to his absent offspring. " I told his mother not to let him come and make his messes in this room. But you know what women are ! "

To this rather large assumption Denny made no reply. His attention was focused upon Mr. Bagby's dispositions for the removal of the ink blot. He was a tidy and methodical man, was Mr. Bagby, and he prided himself on keeping his house in order. There was always an immaculate array of clean towels hanging in the bath-room at Middlefield, and Mr. Bagby's knowledge of the current allowances on returned empties was almost indecent.

Very slowly and stealthily the pink blotting-paper slid over the polished table, until one corner touched the outer edge of the pool of ink.

" This is the awkward bit," said Mr. Bagby breathlessly. " If the ink breaks away now— surface tension, and so on—it will run all over the place ; on the carpet, probably. Stand by with some more blotting-paper, Denny, just in case—— Why, *damn* the thing ! "

For the pink pool did not break away, not even when the blotting-paper, after a moment's hesitation, slid right over its glossy surface ; not even when Mr. Bagby pressed the blotting-paper down with the tip of his finger. The paper still remained a virgin pink.

" Surely the infernal stuff hasn't solidi-fied ! " Mr. Bagby placed the full weight of his palm upon the protuberance ; then, with another regrettable exclamation, snatched the blotting-paper away and began to fumble for his monocle.

The ink pool lay as composed and as unruffled as ever. This was not altogether surprising, for it was composed of black sealing-wax, artistically moulded and varnished.

What Mr. Bagby said when he adjusted his monocle is irrelevant to this narrative, and was fortunately cut short at the very outset by a series of war-whoops of a raucous and pene-trating character which burst from behind a sofa in the corner of the room.

" Ee-ee-ee !   A-a-ah !   Oo-oo-ooh !   Sold

again ! Sold again ! Silly old Bingo ! Sold again ! "

And Master Lionel Bagby, vacating his ambush, shot from the open doorway into the hall and disappeared through a curtained arch on the other side, yodelling triumphantly.

Denny, tactfully leaving the overwrought Mr. Bagby to himself, slipped out of the room after his " chum " and, travelling familiar ground, proceeded down a linoleum-covered passage in the direction of the schoolroom, where he knew that the feast to which he had been invited would be spread. Even as he entered the passage a maid debouched from another doorway, carrying a loaded tray which exuded an agreeable aroma of poached eggs and hot muffins.

Gathered in the schoolroom Denny found Mrs. Bagby herself, present in his honour ; Miss Groves, Gwen's governess ; Lionel the Terrible, still chanting his song of victory ; and the present disturber of his peace, Miss Gwendoline Bagby. Denny shook hands rather shyly all round, that susceptible and elastic organ, his heart, missing a beat or two when he greeted the daughter of the house. Mrs. Bagby took the head, Miss Groves the foot of the table. Master Lionel, who was a dirty feeder and required considerable elbow room, was accommodated with a side to himself. Denny and Gwen sat together.

Mrs. Bagby, having helped the others, addressed her son with an indulgent smile.

" Little Leo," she said, " will you have a poached egg ? "

" Yes," replied Little Leo.

" Yes—what, dear ? "

" What ? An egg, of course. Don't be silly ! "

Mrs. Bagby smiled feebly.

" I am waiting for a certain little word, darling," she said.

" And I," riposted Lionel the Terrible, " am waiting for a certain little poached egg ! "

Mrs. Bagby made another effort.

" If you—— ? " she prompted.

" If you don't give me one," roared Little Leo, in a most threatening voice. " I shall come and take one. So hurry up ! "

Mrs. Bagby, finding the situation, as usual, beyond her, smiled resignedly and passed the egg.

Gwen began to question Denny about his scholarship. When he told her that it was worth sixty pounds a year she was visibly impressed, and Denny turned pink with gratification.

"It doesn't mean much, really," he said modestly.

"What are you going to do with the money?" asked Gwen.

"I don't think you get any money; they just knock sixty pounds off your school bill."

Lionel the Terrible here interposed, to remark that when he won a scholarship he would spend the money on himself and not go to school at all. Having disposed of this topic to his entire satisfaction, he helped himself to jam with an eggy knife.

"What house are you going to, Denis?" asked Miss Groves.

"Keeley's."

Miss Groves's thin face flushed with pleasure.

"My brother was there," she said, "long ago."

"What a rotten house it must have been," observed Little Leo.

As it appeared to be nobody's business to controvert this statement, Miss Groves continued, timidly:

"Of course it was some time ago. My brother has been vicar of Much Moreham for many years now. Will you ask Mr. Keeley if he still remembers him?"

Denny promised to do so, and furthermore undertook to write and tell Miss Groves if

Mr. Keeley did remember her brother. The ice thus artfully broken, he asked if Gwen would like him to write to her too.

"Rather!" said Gwen. "Tell me all your troubles, my child, whenever you feel like it."

"Shall I write to you as well, Leo?" asked Denny, turning away a little dashed.

"No," replied the Terrible One.

"Leo, darling!" interposed his mother.

"No—what?"

"No blooming fear!" explained her offspring. "I should have to read the thing. Hello, here's Bingo!"

The schoolroom door was wrenched open, and the master of the house stood lowering upon the threshold.

"Leo," he announced with an air of intense resolution, "I shall whip you to-night before dinner."

"No you won't," replied his son calmly.

"But I shall!" repeated Mr. Bagby with less conviction.

"No, you won't!" bellowed Lionel the Terrible. Finding his utterance somewhat impeded by bread and jam, he took a large gulp of tea, and continued: "What's the good? It only hurts your hand, and makes me laugh. Look out—you're treading on something!"

There were cries of concern from Mrs. Bagby.

"Ring for Hannah!" she exclaimed. "She must have dropped it off the dish. How careless of her! Don't touch it with your fingers, Miss Groves. Take the coal shovel."

But Miss Groves, who, whatever she might lack in assertiveness, was not deficient in common sense, merely stooped down, picked up the jettisoned poached egg between her finger and thumb, and laid it on the table close beside its engaging proprietor. It really was a capital imitation. The streaming yolk in particular did credit to the designer.

Little Leo was once more bounding about the room.

"Sold again! Sold again!" he yelled. "Silly old Bingo! Silly old Bingo! Sold again!"

*   *   *   *   *

After tea the infant humorist summoned his reluctant guest from the side of his sister, and conducted him upstairs, where he revealed to him the source of his present playful inspirations. It was a Conjurer's Catalogue, entitled *Amusing Jokes and Novel Surprises*.

"You get six jokes in a box for half a crown," he explained. "The poached egg, and the spilt ink thing, and another like spilt jam, and a bandage all bloody that you stick round your

finger to make people think you've cut it—
Gwen fairly blubbed when she saw it on me—
and an imitation wasp, and some india-rubber
bugs you drop into people's soup. The catalogue
says the bugs are also Suitable for Beds. I
haven't used them yet. Half a jiffy! I'll slip
down to the drawing-room now, and put them
on mother's tea-table."

The horrid child sped away, and before Denny
could summon sufficient courage to go back to
the schoolroom in search of Gwen, returned
enraptured, announcing that two beetles now
floated in the cream-jug, while the wasp occupied
a conspicuous position upon the seat which
would shortly be occupied by his father.

" I got a ten-bob tip last week," he continued,
gloating over the catalogue, " and I'm going to
order some more—real spiffers this time. The
first lot were all as stale as anything, but of
course they were quite new to Mum and Bingo.
Here's something. *The Mysterious Voice.
With this little novelty anyone can make the
exact imitation of a kitten mewing, while all
your friends are wondering where it is. Very
amusing and quite new.*' That's rotten. All
you do is to hold a sort of bag in your hand
and squeeze it, or else put it down for someone to sit on. . . . Here's something better.
' The Plush Jewel Case. This little box is in

the form of a small jewel case. When your friend opens it, it gives a loud bang, causing much laughter among the onlookers.' I dare say, but it's two bob. What's this ? ' *The Crash-Bang. This consists of six metal pieces which are thrown against a wall. They give the exact representation of a window being broken. Sixpence.'* I'll get a set of those for Bingo. Hallo ! ' *The Red-Hot Cinder. One of these cinders placed on the hearth-rug causes great consternation, followed by merriment, and calls forth exclamations of " How good ! " when picked up. Fourpence.'* You ought to take some of these to Eaglescliffe with you, Denny. You could rag the masters fearfully."

" I think I'll have a look at the masters first," replied Denny.

Lionel finally settled upon two more purchases —namely, some Nihilist Bombs, " *one of which, exploded in a theatre or railway carriage, will cause people on the spot to gradually get away as far as possible,*" and the Electric Bell—" *which you fasten to a table or wall and ask your friend to ring it. To his great surprise, he pricks his finger. Roars of laughter ! Tenpence* "—and then suggested a visit to the orchard.

Denny, supremely bored, acquiesced. His sole interest in the House of Bagby was centred— and that, as time was to prove, but temporarily

—in the female branch. Besides, the morrow, with its unrevealed and half-feared mysteries, was tugging at his thoughts, rendering him even more impervious than usual to the charms of Little Leo's society. To some of us any company is better than none—which, by the way, accounts for most of the undesirable friendships of this world. Denny was one of the rarer spirits. He desired only the society of the congenial ; failing that, he preferred his own. Such society, at the moment, was represented to him solely by Miss Gwendoline Bagby ; in a few months time he would have revised his standards completely, and be living only for the occasional patronage of brawny youths who could run faster or manipulate a ball more skilfully than himself. But, in the main, Master Denny was a lady's man, as the future will unfold. In other words, he was booked for trouble for many years to come. Meanwhile, his sole preoccupation was a single-minded aversion to the continued society of Little Leo.

However, an apple is seldom amiss when you are thirteen. So he accompanied his host to the orchard. On the way Little Leo espied two beetles scuttling across the gravel path. He picked them up and secured them, with an air of professional secrecy, in an old pill-box.

IN due course that capable young person Joan Cradock piloted her great-uncle back to Abbot's Mill. Here she led the way to the sunny drawing-room on the west side of the house. The room was empty.

"Mother will be here in a moment," said Joan. "I expect she's out with Molly somewhere, as usual. Molly's the pet, you know. Will you have some brandy, or some champagne, or something, till tea is ready? I know where the key of the cellar is."

Sir Anthony declined this hospitable offer, and, straying to the open window, looked out up the river.

"What a landscape!" he said. "Ah me! it's almost worth while living in the Central Provinces of India for the whole of one's working life to revisit such a scene as this occasionally."

"You wait until it rains!" suggested the matter-of-fact Miss Cradock. Sir Anthony laughed.

"My dear, it is possible to live in a country where people *pray* for rain—or rather, would

pray for rain if they knew what it was. But
they don't, so they can't. I come from a place
rather like that. To me a British wet day is
as refreshing as—what shall we say ? "

" Strawberry ice-cream ? "

" Let us say as Balm in Gilead—whatever
that may be. What is that strip of water out
there ? "

" That's Ripleigh Reach. You ought to see
it on a Sunday afternoon," said Joan who, like
most of her sex, was more interested in persons
than places. " Couples in punts come and
moor under those willows all along the bank.
They get so cross if you go near them. Denny
and I have a lot of fun that way."

" What is that island ? "

" That's Abbot's Island."

" It appears to split the river almost evenly."

" Yes. There is a weir on the far side ; the
lock is on this side. Of course that gives
mother fits all day long."

" And why should it give mother fits ? "

" Because she has quite made up her mind
that we are all going to be drowned there some
day. The only thing she hasn't quite settled
is the order of going in. Hallo, here she is !
Now you'll get your tea."

Mildred Cradock, dressed in white, was
approaching from the landing-stage at the foot

of the lawn. For the mother of three lusty children, she looked absurdly young. She was tall and slim, and her figure so far appeared to have escaped that calamity known among the victims as "middle-aged spread." She looked little more than twenty-five, though she was ten years older. Her face beneath her white felt boating-hat was soft and round, and her expression, especially when she looked at her children, both whimsical and tender. She had the easy smile and the comprehending eyes which mark people of a large and tolerant sense of humour. But if you regarded her face closely in a strong light—assuming that you were so ungallant as to do such a thing—you would have observed two little lines running from the curve of each nostril to the corners of her mouth—lines which usually indicate a woman who has had once or twice to set her face resolutely towards the facts of life and practise the art of keeping a stiff upper lip. But the lines were not visible now—nothing but the superficial preoccupation of a con-scientious hostess.

"I hope I haven't kept you waiting for tea, Uncle Tony," she said, as she entered the drawing-room window. "Molly took me out in the punt, and—well, we found the punt-pole a little too long for us, didn't we, Molly?"

She looked down affectionately upon the small figure at her side—a little girl of nine, with a mop of black curly hair, dark blue eyes, and a countenance rendered crimson by recent exertion.

" I did," corrected Molly. She was a literal and truthful child, lacking Joan's worldly poise. Her voice was deeper, too. Altogether Molly took life more seriously than her elder sister.

" The pole stuck in the mud," she announced gravely to Sir Anthony, " and it nearly pulled me in. But mother held on to my frock, and we got it out. Some of the gathers gave way."

" The gathers ? "

" Yes. Look."

Molly turned round, in order to afford her great-uncle a better view of her disordered raiment. Her mother interrupted hastily.

" Now, chick, run off upstairs to your tea, and leave Uncle Tony and me in peace. Take Molly upstairs, Joan."

" Righto ! " replied Joan. " Come on, Mop-head ! I'll race you. You go through the house and I'll go round by the garden."

The challenge was precipitately accepted, and with a wild shriek the two ladies shot out of the door and window respectively, and were no more seen.

Sir Anthony chuckled gently, and sat down in an arm-chair. His hostess, having rung for tea, sat down beside him and took his hand affectionately.

"Dear Uncle Tony," she said, "don't think me a terribly demonstrative female, but you don't know how I enjoy having you here, even for such a flying visit. After all these years, too. I do wish you could stay longer."

"Carried unanimously! But the British Empire must be governed somehow, and sometimes. That reminds me, I have promised to discourse after tea to Joan upon the inner workings of the Indian Civil Service. I think she imagines I black myself all over and listen behind trees to Thugs and Dacoits."

"Don't let her bother you."

"It's a pleasure. Your children are very companionable, Mildred."

Mildred flushed with pleasure. It was easy to see where her treasure was laid up.

"You don't think Joan is too precocious?" she asked, obviously hoping to be contradicted.

"She's got her head screwed on the right way, if that's what you mean. But that doesn't prevent her heart from being in the right place."

"I am glad to hear you say that, because sometimes she seems to me just a little harder

—a little more difficult to mould—than the other two."

" Joan's all right. Her head just about balances the other organ, I should say. In the case of the other two, the balance inclines a little bit towards what magazine editors call ' heart interest '—eh ? They get that from their mother, I imagine."

" What makes you think that ? Do you accuse me of being sentimental ? "

Before Uncle Tony could frame a tactful reply to this leading question, the door opened and a grim-faced maid entered with the tea.

" Out on the veranda, please, Thwaites," said Mildred.

" You'd better have it in here," replied Thwaites calmly.

" But it's quite warm and sunny outside."

" It's September, and a cold in the head is a cold in the head any time of the year. There's your tea. Drink it up while it's hot ; it won't improve with talk." And, having planted the tea-tray on its usual table, Thwaites departed composedly to her own place.

Mildred made a little *moue*.

" You see how I am treated by my staff ! " she said.

" A privileged retainer, I should say."

" You're right ; she is. She was my maid

in the old days. When I became the mother of
a growing family a maid looked like an extravagance, so I turned her into a parlourmaid.
She wages perpetual warfare with the children,
but they love one another really."

" She was with you before your marriage ? "

" Yes."

" Then she knew your husband ? "

" Yes. Sugar and cream, Uncle Tony ? "

" No, thank you. I wish I'd known him too.
Do you care to speak of him, or do you prefer
to keep your memories to yourself ? "

" No," said Mildred after a pause. " I think
I like to speak of him. Of course, to a certain
extent one's memories are sacred things, but
that is no reason why one should not recall
them for other people. Denis is a mere name
to you, naturally."

" Yes. I heard in a vague way in India,
fifteen years ago, that you had gone out to
South Africa, and that you had married there ;
but the first definite news that I had was your
cable asking me to be Master Denny's godfather."

" Yes. He was born on the second of July.
He weighed——"

" Tell me about the other Denis—your husband," said Uncle Tony, a little hastily.

Mildred obediently abandoned nursery statistics,

B

and her face assumed a curious rapt and far away expression. She began to talk in a low monotone—like a medium describing a vision. Apparently the memories she recalled were written deeply on her heart.

" I was in Cape Town," she began, " when the South African War broke out, staying at the Mount Nelson Hotel."

" Alone ? "

" Yes."

" How old were you ? "

" Just twenty-one."

" God bless my soul ! "

" I had gone there to get away from—— "

" An undesirable suitor in London ? "

" Yes. But he wasn't undesirable—only rather stupid."

" But he was pertinacious ? "

" Yes. And being a girl of independent disposition—— "

" You certainly were. I remember your swimming out to the bell-buoy at Whiteness and back when you were barely seventeen, just because somebody bet you you couldn't."

" Fancy your remembering that ! "

" I always remember important things. Continue. Of independent disposition—— ? "

" ——And just having come into my money, I thought it would be a good plan to leave

England, and—and—see the world. So I told
the other two trustees—old Mr. Embury and
General Oddie—since you weren't there—— "

" I certainly was not, or there would have
been a little more opposition, I promise you ! "

" I told them what I meant to do. They
were terribly upset ; but seeing that I was
determined, they gave way. So Thwaites and
I packed up—you can imagine Thwaites's
comments on the excursion !—and went off to
Cape Town together. There we were caught by
the South African War."

" And couldn't get back—eh ? "

" I am not sure that I wanted to. I went
and worked in Wynberg Hospital. I was quite
happy there. You see, I was doing something
useful for the first time in my life. There
I met—Denis. He was one of my first patients."

Sir Anthony nodded comprehendingly.

" A wounded officer—eh ? Have you a
photograph of him ? "

" No. But he was a very handsome man."

" What was his regiment ? "

" Somebody's Irregular Horse, I think. I am
always rather stupid about military titles. We
were married almost at once—as soon as
he was convalescent. He wasn't seriously
wounded, and we lived in Cape Town for nearly
four years."

" Didn't he go back to duty ? "

" No. I think he had a job at the Base given him. . . . Anyhow, the war ended at last."

" And you sailed for home ? "

" Not immediately. Denis had various business interests in Cape Town, and he could not get out of them all at once. The war had been over nearly a year before we sailed. I had little Denny and Joan with me, of course ; Molly wasn't born until a few months later."

" You sailed on the *Gallia*."

Mildred nodded. " You remember what happened, then ? " she said.

" One read about it in the newspapers, of course. Collided with another boat, didn't she ? "

" Yes—one terribly dark night off Teneriffe. We nearly cut her in two ; and we began to sink as well. It was pretty awful."

" A sad business. What were your own experiences ? "

" I was very helpless at the time ; but everybody was wonderful to me. They put me into one of the biggest boats, with the two children. We were picked up by another ship the next day, not much the worse."

" And your husband ? "

Mildred Cradock drew a long, full breath, and

once again her face assumed the same fixed, rapt expression.

"The last glimpse I had of him," she said, "he was saving someone else's life. I never set eyes on him again—after that."

Her voice ran down, with a little quivering sigh. There was a pause. Then Sir Anthony said gently:

"At least he left a gallant memory behind him."

"You are right, Uncle Tony; that is just what he did leave." Mildred was speaking with a curious intensity now, and the little drawn lines in the corners of her mouth were visible. "And that memory has been my sheet-anchor to windward for nearly ten years. While he was alive it was strength to be with him; now that he has gone it is strength to remember him. I don't pretend to be a strong woman, or a clever woman; so when I am in any doubt or difficulty about myself or the children, I just say to myself: What would Denis have done about it? That's been a real help, Uncle Tony."

"I can quite believe it, my dear."

"And I try to bring up my children by his standard—that's all. Now, I mustn't bother you any more." She rose, smiling hospitably, with a woman's enviable faculty for shaking off a grave topic. " Come into the garden and smoke a cigar."

" I will," replied Sir Anthony. He rose, and laid his hand upon his niece's shoulder. " But tell me one thing : can I help you or serve you in any way ? I hesitate to offer, because you are the most competent woman I have ever met. But as you have got an odd man about the house for a week or so, you might as well make use of him. Can I do anything ? Audit your pass-book ? Have a row with the plumber ? Whitewash the henhouse ? I am yours to command."

" I'll tell you what you can do, Uncle Tony," said Mildred suddenly. " Have a talk with Denny. Give him some advice."

Uncle Tony made a wry face.

" H'm ! An improving discourse to a young man about to leave home for the first time—eh ? It's a bit out of my line. In my own circle I fear I am regarded as a rather worldly, not to say cynical, old gentleman."

" You are nothing of the kind."

" Well, I'll admit I impose on some people— Joan, for instance. She regards me as some- thing between a newly-born babe and a doddering octogenarian—which I suppose, when you come to think of it, I am. In fact, we all are. However, I'll try. After all, the boy's my godson—and I fairly asked for it. I'll do it now. Where is he ? "

" He's at a tea-party at Middlefield, with his friend Leo Bagby."

" And Miss Bagby, I gathered."

" From Joan, of course ? "

" Joan was certainly my informant."

" Joan's an imp. But never mind that. Why not talk to him when he comes home this evening, about six o'clock ? "

" That hour is already bespoke by the young lady just mentioned. I'll tell you what. I'll stroll over to Middlefield now, and meet him. Then I can get things off my chest on the way home."

" Will you ? How kind you are to me ? "

" Isn't everybody ? "

" Well, now I come to think of it, I suppose everybody is."

" They ought to be. You are the nicest woman I know. *Au revoir !* Exit Admonitory Uncle. Tell Joan I will be back in good time."

The door closed, and Sir Anthony's footsteps died away in the direction of the front door. Mildred crossed to a little table beside the fire-place. Upon it stood three photographs —one of each of her children. One by one she picked them up and examined them. She

lingered a little longer over Molly than the
others. Suddenly the door behind her opened,
and Thwaites appeared. Mildred guiltily set
down Molly's photograph and turned towards
the window. Thwaites began to collect the
tea-things.

" Some people," she observed severely, " don't
know when they're well off."

Mildred did not reply. She stood gazing
out towards the river ; but she did not see it,
for her eyes were filled with tears.

I

SHORTLY before six o'clock Uncle Tony presented himself at Middlefield, where he experienced no difficulty whatever in persuading his godson that it was time to come home.

Mr. Bagby, who had recently fished two india-rubber beetles out of the cream-jug, besides devoting some breathless moments to the stalking of a wasp which ultimately proved to be made of cotton-wool, surveyed the departing Denny and his escort with something like a sigh.

"Fancy getting a boy off one's hands for three whole months," he observed enviously. Then he turned to his wife.

"Look here, Constancia"—he had propounded this question before, invariably to his own discomfiture, but hope springs eternal—"why shouldn't we send that little devil to school too?"

Mrs. Bagby shook her head mournfully.

"I could not bear it," she said. "It would

take all the sunshine out of the house. One day, perhaps, we will put his name down for some really nice school—but not yet. It would kill me."

"Why not send him to Eaglescliffe," suggested Mr. Bagby. "That's a great school, if you like. Denny Cradock will be there too."

"When my Leo goes to school," replied Mrs. Bagby, swelling a little, "he must consort with boys of his own station. Denny Cradock is well enough here; but it might stand in Leo's way if they went into a larger world together. You see, Denny is going to school as a sort of charity-boy, while our son will be paying his way."

Mr. Bagby groaned softly, and acquiesced. It is useless to explain to an uneducated and purse-proud woman that open scholarships are not awarded by our public schools for sweet charity's sake. So Mr. Bagby dropped the subject, as he always did, merely hoping that one day his son would over-reach himself.

And already the hour of deliverance was at hand. Even as they conversed, the Sunshine of the House was creeping stealthily up the staircase behind their backs, holding a battered pill-box in his hand. Though he did not know it, Lionel the Terrible was going to his Moscow. At half-past seven Mrs. Bagby went upstairs to dress for dinner. No maid was visible, so the mistress, having rung the bell with some asperity, sat down before her dressing-table and began to take off her rings. While engaged in this task she became aware, through the reflection of her mirror, that the bed behind her did not present its usual smooth and un-ruffled appearance. She turned and subjected it to direct scrutiny.

The counterpane gave the impression of having been turned back and then replaced by someone unskilled in the art of bed-making. Almost exactly in the centre a small hump was noticeable.

Mrs. Bagby, shrewdly suspecting a fresh instance of the playfulness of her inventive son, decided at first to allow her maid to investigate the mystery. Then, curiosity proving too strong for her, she rose to her feet and cautiously turned back the bedclothes.

In the very heart of the bed, between the two sheets, she came upon a neat ring-fence, or zareba, some six inches in diameter, composed of two tortoise-shell side-combs. In the middle of the enclosure lay two beetles.

Mrs. Bagby, repressing a perfectly natural start of disgust, removed the combs and restored them to the dressing-table. Then a thought struck her. Should she call her husband? she wondered. For him the spectacle of his delicately nurtured wife removing india-rubber beetles from her bed with a nonchalant and indulgent smile would be a capital object lesson in the proper method of dealing with the pranks of a high-spirited and lovable child. Yes, she would summon him. No, he would probably be washing himself. She would take the beetles to him.

Certainly they were very life-like insects—almost as convincing as the pair that her son had left in the cream-jug.

She picked them up.

One of the beetles immediately fell out of her hand on to the bed, and scuttled in an agitated fashion under a lace-trimmed pillow. The other, without the slightest hesitation, ran straight up Mrs. Bagby's sleeve.

2

Meanwhile, Denny and his godfather were walking home across the fields.

" Did you enjoy your party, Denny? " asked Uncle Tony.

" I had a jolly good tea."

" Is that your only comment? "

Denny nodded.

" From that elliptical response I gather that Master Lionel was in form."

"Yes. He was beastly rude to his mother and Miss Groves. I nearly scragged his head once or twice."

"But you didn't?"

"No." Denny looked up and laughed. "Perhaps it's just as well I didn't try. He's a stone heavier than I am."

"Still, I know your mother will be pleased with you for going over to say good-bye. I hope, by the way, that you were rewarded in another quarter."

Denny reddened.

"Oh, that's just some rot of Joan's," he said; and then continued, as one anxious to change the subject:

"It was awfully decent of you to come over and walk home with me, Uncle Tony."

"My dear Denny, don't thank me. I am simply revelling in my newly-found privileges. For a crusty old bachelor to come home from the East after many years and find not only a long-lost niece, but a ready-made contingent of jolly grand-nephews and grand-nieces all waiting to make much of him and spoil him— well, I don't require any thanks, thank you!"

"You aren't old or crusty, really!" replied Denny politely.

"I am sixty-three, Denny; and as for crustiness—you ought to see me in my Club,

bundling junior members out of my pet arm-
chair and throwing chutney at the head waiter!
Of course I am on my good behaviour here.
Now, after this more than Oriental exchange
of compliments, let me ask you something.
Would you like me, or your mother, or both
of us, to come with you to Eaglescliffe on
Thursday, or would you rather go alone?"

"I'll go alone," replied Denny, speaking
more boldly than he felt.

"I think you're right. Head first, and no
shivering on the brink—that's the only way
to tackle the unknown. There's no blinking
the fact, Denny, that leaving home and its
intimacies and finding your feet in strange
surroundings calls for a certain resolution.
You'll be up against a similar experience again
and again during life—going up to the Varsity,
or going to Sandhurst as a cadet, or walking
into your regimental mess for the first time,
or facing a row of supercilious fellow-clerks
in an office; or, for that matter, tackling a
week-end at a country house full of critical
eyes and artificial complexions. It's a pros-
pect we have to anticipate all our lives.
One gets hardened to it in time, and each
experience is a little easier than the last. So
when you go to school next week and feel like
a strange cat at a dog show, as you will for

a while, always remember that you have to begin some time, and that it is never going to be as difficult again."

Denny took his godfather's arm and squeezed it. He was nearly fourteen, but he was a very little boy in some ways.

"Of course," continued Uncle Tony, divining that his godson was more in the mood to listen than to talk, "if your mother were to go down to Eaglescliffe with you she would make things considerably easier, in a way. She always does—always did. She would captivate the Head, and Mr. Keeley, and the Matron, and the Porter, and go away leaving every one as pleased with themselves as anything, and quite unwarrantably pre-possessed in your favour. Then you would have to live all that down, and begin by yourself. No, I think you're right to go alone. I'll tell you what, though. Your mother and I will run up to town with you on Thursday and stand you lunch, and then we'll see you off from Waterloo."

"Thank you," said Denny. Then came the confidence that had been trembling upon his lips for ten minutes.

"I'm afraid I shall do an awful lot of idiotic things at first—through not knowing."

"I sincerely hope so."

Denny looked up, surprised.

" Why ? "

" Because every time we make what is known as a bloomer, we learn something. The man who sits back and never asks a foolish question never gets anywhere, under any circumstances. Denny, promise me something."

" Rather, Uncle Tony ! "

" At least half of this globe is peopled by folk whose chief joy in life is to impart information ; so don't disappoint them. They will teach you all you want to know, and gladly, for nothing, if you will let them. The failures of humanity are the people who were too proud and too shy to admit that they did not *know ;* so nobody told them. It's a terrible thing to go through life, or through a conversation, for that matter, looking intensely knowing, yet knowing nothing. Promise me that when you don't know you won't pretend that you do ! "

" Righto ! Uncle Tony," replied Denny politely.

Uncle Tony surveyed his godson whimsically.

" Yes," he said, " you're right ! Advice is what the old give to the young when they're too decayed to profit by it themselves. This *is* an improving discourse from Great Uncle ! But I promised to deliver it, and it's nearly over. There's one other thing. Don't be

ashamed of being enthusiastic. Affected in-
difference is the curse of our nation. Up to a
point it's all right ; it fits in with our inborn
hatred of advertisement. But we overdo it.
When we fail in some cherished undertaking
we pretend we don't care ; and when we
succeed we pretend it was a fluke. That
attitude has deluded many a gallant but
simple soul into believing that nothing really
matters. Well, everything matters. *Keen,
clear, clean!* That's the curler's motto—and
a pretty good one too, especially for people
who are inclined to retire into their shell when
snubbed or criticised—people like you and me.
That's all, I think, for the present. There
is another topic, but it will keep—say, until
you're twenty-one . . .

" You'll enjoy Eaglescliffe, once the plunge
is over. You won't *learn* anything there, of
course : English public schools are not conducted to that end. But if you acquire the
habit of speaking the truth, obeying a legitimate order without arguing, and accepting
responsibility as a matter of course—remember
we're an Imperial race—you'll have graduated
with honours. And if ever you find yourself
at any time confronted with the question :
' What would a gentleman do ? ' allow me to
direct your attention to the Fifteenth Psalm.

Hallo, there's Joan waiting for us. How she would laugh if she knew what we were talking about. Let us abandon these schoolboy confidences, and become cynical and witty for the benefit of the fair sex!"

It is no easy matter to organise a successful
up-river picnic. You require fine weather; you
require catering experience; and you require
tact—especially tact. The problem of the fox
and the goose and the bundle of hay—by the
way, do geese eat hay?—is child's play compared with the task that confronts a hostess
called upon to divide a punt, a Canadian canoe,
and a motor-launch among a party of assorted
ages and sexes.

However, by steadfastly bearing in mind:

1. That Mrs. Bagby would decline to trust
herself to anything but the motor-launch;

2. That Denny's last afternoon at home
would be entirely wrecked unless he got Gwen
to himself in the canoe either going or returning;

3. That Lionel the Terrible must be segre-
gated from all persons of refined or fastidious
disposition;

4. That if Lionel and his father were placed
in the same boat there would certainly be a riot,
and probably a shipwreck—

Mildred finally sent her party forth as follows:

In the motor-launch were Mr. and Mrs. Bagby, Sir Anthony and Joan. Mildred went in the punt herself, accompanied by Molly and Lionel the Terrible. This left the canoe free for Denny and Gwen.

Thus manned, the flotilla set off up Ripleigh Reach, headed by the motor-launch, which naturally landed at the landing point comparatively quickly, to the undisguised relief of Joan who, with Sir Anthony, had found the bickerings of Mr. and Mrs. Bagby more than a little trying. The punt came next, not unskilfully piloted by Little Leo, surprisingly docile under the calm, compelling providence that lurked behind Mildred Cradock's smiling face. Denny and Gwen arrived a bad third, Denny dumbly worshipping, the young lady frankly bored.

Presently the feast was spread, and after Little Leo had been frustrated in an attempt to plant the butter where his male parent would indubitably have sat upon it, the revels commenced. The guests of honour were Denny and Leo, for the latter was going to school too. The episode of the beetles had given Mr. Bagby the chance of a lifetime; and before Mrs. Bagby had revived sufficiently from nervous prostration to resume her normal attitude of sentimental obstructiveness to all schemes for her son's reformation, that indignant youth had been telegraphically offered to and telephonically accepted by the authorities of Eaglescliffe School, who found themselves with an unexpected vacancy in Mr. Keeley's house at the last moment. However, he did not allow the approaching severance of home ties to affect his appetite. Indeed, it is probable that he enjoyed the picnic more than anyone else.

Truth to tell, it was not a particularly hilarious function. Mrs. Bagby, as became her, was in the depth of woe at the thought of her coming bereavement. Mr. Bagby, whose heart was like a singing-bird at the same idea, deemed it wiser to assume a demeanour of Spartan resignation. Miss Gwendoline Bagby, who was approaching the age at which the attendance of one or more presentable adult youths would have been welcome, maintained the pose of a society queen compelled to patronise a school-treat.

So much for the Bagbys. As for the Cradocks, Joan was taciturn but observant, Molly was inclined to be a little tearful over Denny, while Denny was sentimentally engrossed with Gwen. Uncle Tony, whom long experience had trained to take life as he found it, sat upon a folded newspaper smoking a cigar, and hoping for nothing worse on the morrow than a slight stiffness of the joints. Mildred Cradock alone

seemed to be enjoying herself. But then she
always did : everybody knew that.

" A pleasant, fluffy, feminine creature without
any knowledge or appreciation of the deeper
issues of life, but well-meaning and hospitable,
in a fussy sort of way," was the verdict of the
parish, as expressed by the parish oracle, Miss
Laura Meakin, Mildred's nearest neighbour.
The picnic, by the way, had narrowly escaped the
honour of that lady's attendance. Not that she
had been invited, but the omission would have
been pardoned and the invitation taken for
granted in any case. That is the sort of person
Laura was. However, to-day she was absent, an
emergency meeting of the committee of some
society for the curtailment of other people's
personal liberty—an enterprise in which she
was perennially interested—having called her
to an adjacent parish.

Still, tea in itself is always a pleasant function,
and up-river picnics are not the penitential
feasts that they once were.

" The invention of the Thermos flask," observed
Uncle Tony, " has lightened the labours and
brightened the life of many an arthritic fuel-
gatherer ; and the tea itself no longer tastes
like a decoction of dead leaves and tepid pond
water. May I pass my cup up again, Mildred ? "

" The midges are very bad," complained

Mrs. Bagby. "Leo, darling, don't scratch the place. It will only irritate your skin."

"I like scratching," replied the Terror simply : and continued to do so.

"Leo, sir, obey your mother at once!" thundered Mr. Bagby.

"Oh, shut up, Bingo!" retorted the amiable child.

"Supposing," interposed Mildred, "when we have cleared the tea-things, we get into the boats again and drift home. We needn't hurry, of course, but there will be fewer midges on the water. Let me see now. How shall we distribute ourselves this time?" She cast a guileless but calculating eye upon the motley assemblage before her.

"I wonder what time it is," said Mrs. Bagby.

"Twenty-five to seven," replied Denny, with a careless glance at his new wrist-watch.

"Oh dear, I didn't know it was so late! I must get home at once. I like to give myself a full hour to dress in the evening."

"I am so sorry," said Mildred. "I would have warned you sooner if I had known. Suppose you take your own launch, and leave my little band to follow in the boats. We are in no hurry : we are only going back to a cold supper."

"We," announced Little Leo with simple dignity, "are going back to a hot dinner. We have one every night. Let's start now. Come on, Bingo ; get a move on ! "

An hour later the punt and the canoe, relieved of the ostentatious companionship of the motor-launch, were drifting amicably down Ripleigh Reach, within easy conversational distance of one another, in the gloaming of a September evening. Uncle Tony and Joan shared the canoe, while Mildred, with Molly's head in her lap, reclined restfully in the punt, whose course her son, seated in the stern, was lazily directing with a paddle.

Molly's gruff little voice was heard uplifted in affectionate entreaty.

" She's asking Mother to tell her a story," Joan announced to her grand-uncle. " And I bet I know which one it is."

" Is your mother's repertoire so limited ? "

" Oh, no ; only Molly always wants the same old stale things. I expect to-night it will be the one about—hallo ! "

Mrs. Cradock was speaking.

" Shall I tell you a new one, for once—since Denny is going away ? "

" All right," agreed Molly, a little reluctantly.

" I have always meant to tell it to you some time. It isn't very long." Mildred turned to her son. " But it's for you to choose to-night,

Denny. Would you rather listen to a story, or shall we just drift, and chat?"

"I think I'd rather listen to a story," replied Denny, in an unusually subdued voice.

"Very well, then. Once upon a time"—Mildred Cradock's steady voice came drifting across the water to the canoe with surprising clearness—"a great ship was sailing along at night, not far from the West Coast of Africa. She was homeward bound——"

"Where from?" inquired Molly, greedy for detail, as usual.

"From South Africa, where a war was just over."

"Ah!" remarked Uncle Tony to himself. Joan looked up.

"South Africa was where I was born," she observed. "Mother has a lot of stories about it."

"The ship," continued Mildred, "was full of soldiers, going home to their wives and babies. Some of them had their wives and babies with them, because the war had been over for nearly a year. Well, the babies were all fast asleep in their cots, and their mothers were getting ready to go to theirs too, when suddenly there came a cry and a crash in the darkness. People came running up on deck——"

"Was it a rock," inquired Molly breathlessly, "or a submarine?"

" It wasn't either. Submarines weren't invented in those days—were they, Denny ? "

" No, mother, I don't think so."

" There was a thick fog, and the look-out men could scarcely see, though they peered and peered through the fog and darkness. There was a great commotion, and presently it was known what had happened. They had run into a little steamboat."

" How big was she ? "

" Well, she was a boat that carried coals."

" A collier ? " suggested Denny learnedly.

" Yes, that is just what she was. She was sinking fast, and so was the big ship, for there was a great big hole in the bow where she had struck the other. However, the sea was not too rough, and everybody was very brave. The soldiers took their places on the deck, standing in straight lines and waiting for their officers to tell them what to do. The order was given to lower the boats and put the passengers into them. There were—other passengers besides the soldiers."

" Women and children first, of course," said Denny.

" Yes, certainly ; then the others ; the soldiers last."

" Did everybody get off ? " asked Molly, still rushing her fences.

" Yes."

" All the soldiers as well ? "

Mildred appeared to hesitate for a moment, then she answered :

" Yes—nearly all, I think. But the story isn't really about the big ship, because she went down almost immediately, poor thing. It's just about one of the boats—a boat so crowded with women and children that they had to pass some of them into another boat which was not so full. There was a little girl in the crowded boat, Molly—rather like you."

" I suppose it *wasn't* me ? " inquired Molly hoping against hope.

" Oh, dear, no. You weren't born in those days."

" Scored off ! " remarked Joan, *sotto voce*, to her grand-uncle.

" She was just a little girl in a white frock— the littlest of all the ship's company. She had become separated from her mother, so they tried to pass her over into the boat where her mother was. They had almost done it when a great wave surged up between the boats and swept them apart."

" But what happened to the little *girl* ? "

" She dropped between the boats and went under, out of sight."

" O-o-oh ! " Molly's deep groan of dismay

was a sterling tribute to her mother's powers of narration. However, Mildred continued quickly :

" Directly after that the boats swung together again in the trough of a wave. But just before they closed, a man in one of them sprang up and dived over the side, into the gap between ? "

" Did he save her ? Did he ? "

" Yes. Next time the boats swung apart, there he was, with the little girl in his arms. He held her up, and they lifted her on board and gave her back to her mother."

" Oo-oo-ooh ! " exclaimed Molly. There is a world of difference between the expressions " Ooh ! " and " Oh ! "

" But just as they were reaching out hands to help him, he slipped down under the boat out of sight ; and when the boat was moved over he was gone. They—they didn't see him again." Mildred's voice shook a little. " They thought perhaps he must have struck his head against something."

" A bit of wreckage, perhaps," said Denny.

" Yes—driftwood. All he had strength for was to hold up the child for a moment. He could save others, but not himself."

It was quite dark now. There came a long pause, while the punt, under Denny's silent guidance, drifted down stream another hundred yards or so. Not far away Uncle Tony's glowing cigar indicated the proximity of the canoe; but even Joan was silent. It was Molly who broke the spell at last.

" Mother, you don't often tell us sad stories."

" No, dear."

" But I know why you told us this one."

" Why ? "

" Because you knew the man ! "

Mildred bent over her small daughter's upturned face.

" Did I, dear ? "

" Yes. I don't know who he was; but you knew him, and you wanted us to know about him."

" I believe she's right, for once," commented Joan.

" Who was he, mother ? " asked Denny, leaning forward.

Mildred Cradock drew a deep breath.

" He was your father," she said.

cigar indicated the proximity of the range

Chapter VI   A Page of Unwritten History

PALM BEACH, Florida, is one of the pleasantest
spots on earth—for about a fortnight. After
that you are conscious of an intense desire to
get up and go out and do something useful
and grubby—trim coal, or scrape a boiler, or
sweep a crossing—anything, in fact, which
will relieve you from the sensation of being
an entirely useless cumberer of the ground.
But during that fortnight, provided that you
are in genuine need of a holiday and are staying
there at someone else's expense, you will find
Palm Beach as near an approach to the Elysian
Fields as one can reasonably expect in this
imperfect world. But you must be careful to
drink fairly deep of the water of Lethe first.

The quality which distinguishes Palm Beach
from rival establishments is that its pleasures
are not purely local or indigenous. Practically
everything that ministers to human enjoyment
is to be found there, and everything is just
right. In the first place, the weather is guaran-
teed. It never rains, except for a cooling
shower when everybody is comfortably in

bed. All day long a semi-tropical sun shines out, tempered by a slight sea breeze ; by night a moon, looking about as big as a bass drum in a jazz band, makes a regular appearance. It is always there. The moon in Florida never seems to have a night off at all ; perhaps they keep a spare one.

What is the next requirement of a perfect pleasure resort ? Congenial occupation ? Well, Palm Beach will furnish all your wants. Are you nautically inclined ? You can charter a sailing boat, or more probably a motor-launch, and drop down the coast some seventy miles to Miami—pronounced locally " My Ammer " —whence you can lose yourself among the Florida Keys, a great chain of fairy islands, some no larger than osier beds, strung out southward for a hundred miles. You can wander in and out of winding channels, picturesquely named—Cæsar Creek, Fairy Creek, Jewfish Creek —landing here, bathing there, camping where it pleases you ; for the sea is always calm and the warm water is never more than six feet deep. You can see the white sandy bottom every time you glance over the side of the boat. Of course this is only fair-weather yachting, but life at Palm Beach is only fair-weather life.

Do you require exercise ? There are admirable tennis courts, whither some of the best

tennis players in the world are glad to be invited ;
and there is a golf course. It is not a good
golf course ; but the beauty about golf is that
the worse the course the more golf you get out
of it.

Or if you lean to the really strenuous life,
you can try ocean fishing. In the cold and
ungenerous seas that batter our native shores
we have herrings a few inches long, which we
catch by the thousand in nets ; but off the coast
of Florida, in the warm waters of the Gulf
Stream, you can encounter the same creature
swollen to pantomimic proportions, which you
can only detach from its element by turning
yourself into a human derrick. Even then
your quarry, which is called a tarpon, is quite
capable of shouldering your boat out of the
water. And there are other kinds, smaller fry
some forty or fifty pounds in weight—amber-
jack, barracoota, muttonfish—names suggestive
of " Alice in Wonderland " or " The Bad Child's
Book of Beasts," but real fish and sturdy fighters
for all that.

Or perhaps you are in search of rest and
privacy. Palm Beach is one of the few spots
upon the American Continent where you can
get either—or what passes for either in that
great and busy land. The journey from New
York alone occupies two nights and a day, while

accommodation is, or was a few years ago, limited to two giant hotels, a number of seaside " cottages," so-called, and a couple of clubs which you must belong to or be socially dead. This means that society is limited to a body of some few hundred people who either all know one another or, which is far better, know all about one another.* Palm Beach witnesses the Federal consummation of all the high social mysteries of the United States and Canada. Here Newport mingles with the North Shore, and Michigan Boulevard fraternises with the Mount Royal Club. There is neither space nor atmosphere for the typical American holiday-maker, who, like the British prototype, is a gregarious animal and likes to do things to full band accompaniment. There are no popular amusements at Palm Beach, no peanut stands, no corner drug stores ; there is not even a picture palace. The shops are few and of the bijou variety, tiny offshoots of more pretentious establishments in New York—one sees the same ephemeral little spiders' parlours at Cannes or Deauville—where you may purchase a jumper, or a bathing dress, or a box of candy for little more than twice the metropolitan figure.

And, above all, there are no Conventions.

*The period described is early 1917. Palm Beach has grown since then.

C

But first let us be clear as to what a Convention
is. In England the conventions are unwritten
rules and regulations which you defy or conform to according to your sense of humour.
But a Convention in America is a concrete,
living, palpitating fact. In England we should
call it a Conference, or a Beanfeast, or a blend
of both—something between the British Associa-
tion and the Annual Picnic of the Hearts of
Oak Benefit Society. A Convention is a co-
operative outing upon a vast scale, confined
to commercial or professional gentlemen all of
one calling—the Automobile Salesmen of the
Cincinnati District, or the Fraternity of Adver-
tising Dentists of the State of Minnesota. These
mobilise once a year and descend upon some
chosen and appropriate spot to celebrate their
own existence with feasting and song. They
are addicted to badges, buttons, and, occasionally, distinctive headgear. They hold banquets,
where they indulge in incredible passion for
oratory. They move about chiefly in procession.
They take an entire theatre for a night and go
there *en masse*. Usually they have some slogan
or war-cry of their own, and when they feel like
it they halt and deliver it in chorus, regardless
of the presence of the laity.

American Conventions resort mainly to such
holiday centres as Atlantic City, and Atlantic

City receives them with open arms. They galvanise the place with their enormous vitality, their remorseless bonhomie, and their whole-hearted absorption in the matter in hand—the promotion of Big Business, and the general boosting of their own particular Brotherhood.

But Palm Beach is not for these—at least, not yet. You may traverse that haunt of artificial peace from end to end for a day and a night without once hearing the words " Pep," or " Publicity," or " Hundred per cent. Efficiency," or " Red-Blooded Americanism " uttered, or even whispered. And in the United States of America that is Privacy, that is Tranquillity, if you like !

* * * * *

Still, few of the visitors to Palm Beach are really in search of repose ; they are there to plunge into what is known as the social whirl. In that case, whether you are in society, or merely standing round and watching it, you will find your day pretty fully occupied.

You will probably begin, after a light breakfast in the open air, by proceeding to the beach in a species of wickerwork perambulator—shared, possibly, with Something rather Decorative and propelled by a discreet Ethiopian perched upon a sort of tricycle behind—along

an asphalt pathway which winds by the borders
of a calm lagoon, beneath coco-nut palms.
The next two hours you will devote to bathing
in glorious surf, or basking upon the sand in
an enclosed portion of the beach where everybody knows everybody else and the daily tide
of gossip is beginning to run strongly.

About half-past twelve comes the hour of
the first *apéritif*—in other words, cocktail-time
at The Breakers Hotel. (Yes, all the world
knows that America is now bone dry ; but news
travels slowly in Florida.) After that you will
lunch, quite quietly—probably at some informal gathering of not more than fifteen or
twenty guests in some one's " cottage "—or at
a delightful establishment known as The
Everglades Club.

So far the social whirl has followed an un-
deviating orbit ; but after luncheon tangents
are permitted. You may play a mixed four-
some at golf, or tennis, or bridge, or you may
content yourself with looking on at these
strenuous diversions ; or you may be perfectly
frank and retire to bed for a most acceptable
siesta.

The day is born again at five o'clock, just
as the soft tropical darkness rushes down from
the cloudless sky. (Remember, it is only
February.) All the world assembles round a

clearing in the Cocoanut Grove, and that solemn
mystery Tea is celebrated.

Afternoon tea is a curious meal. In England,
the land of its birth, it is without honour ;
people drink it standing up, sitting down, or
walking about—at a table, at a desk, or off
the corner of the mantelpiece ; sometimes it
is merely imbibed from a thermos flask in the
back office. No Englishman or Scotsman really
cares where or how he has his Tea, so long as
he gets it. But when Tea crosses the ocean
and becomes an imported custom, it is invested
with a strange and unseemly pomp. Foreigners
have missed the point of Tea, which is that it
is above all things a hugger-mugger affair.
Because the Englishman would rather perish
than go without it, the Frenchman and American
conclude that some mystic importance attaches
to the liquid—something that goes down to the
roots of the British constitution—something
which demands libations, and possibly an in-
cantation or two. So the Frenchman puts on
his best clothes to drink it, and calls it The
Five O'Clock. In America—America proper,
west of the Alleghanies—if your hostess, in
the kindness of heart, sets out to prepare you
a cup, she does so with the preoccupied solemnity
of a chemist making up a prescription or an
astrologer compounding a love potion ; and

the resulting decoction is very much what you would expect. And yet not. That is the strange part of it. We rough islanders shovel half a dozen spoonfuls into an old brown tea-pot, fill up the same from the kettle, and the result is at least adequate every time. All you can foretell with safety about the same beverage when prepared by an alien hand, however friendly, is that it will never be the same thing twice. Of course there is another alternative. In the breakfast-car upon the trains that run to the West, if you ask for tea, as often as not your attendant Afreet will dump upon your table a one-ounce packet of tea, an empty teapot, and a small jug of tepid water, and leave you with an indulgent smile to perform the "big juju" for yourself. No wonder that in America Englishmen drink coffee—for the same reason that in England Americans drink tea.

In the Cocoanut Grove the ceremonial per-formance of the Tea rite is still further com-plicated. If you want Tea you must dance for it—upon the great open-air floor, beneath the early evening stars and the ruby electric lights threaded from palm to palm. But this com-plication has no terrors for the assembled com-pany. American men all dance at least passably well, probably because, unlike Englishmen, they are not ashamed to go and learn; while

American girls appear to dance by nature. So the Marimba band plays softly, and you sit and sip your tea to the whispering of innumerable feet and the soothing drone of gossip, now rising to high-water mark.

After this, the sexes separate until dinnertime. Then, if you desire to graduate with the highest social honours, you must dine at the so-called Beach Club—more familiarly, Bradley's—an establishment so restricted in its accommodation that the feat of engaging a table there at all confers a certain *cachet* in itself. After dinner comes a little roulette, in the adjoining rooms—and for no mean stakes, either. Of course to play games of chance in public in any part of the United States is illegal—as illegal as it is in England. More illegal ; for in certain States the Law says that you may not play for money even in the privacy of your own home-circle. Still, the thing is done.

To explain this apparent lapse from upright citizenship requires a certain understanding of the American Constitution. The American moral code is probably the highest in existence —certainly much higher than in our own Laodicean island. More pleasant sins are prohibited in America than anywhere else on earth. The Uplifters—and their name is legion, especially outside the great cities—are able to point to this fact with legitimate pride. Then how is it possible to play roulette at Palm Beach ?

Well, do you remember what Ko-ko said to the Mikado when caught issuing a false death-certificate ?

" It's like this. When your Majesty says, ' Let a thing be done,' it's as good as done. Practically it *is* done, because your Majesty's will is law. Your Majesty says, ' Kill a gentle-man,' and a gentleman is told off to be killed. Consequently that gentleman is as good as dead. Practically he *is* dead. And if he is dead—why not say so ? "

That is how the unregenate section of the American community talk to the numerically superior, overwhelmingly superior, Army of Uplift—and get away with it !

However, if you do not approve of gambling (having lost all your money already) you will probably devote the evening to dancing— dancing everywhere, anywhere After that you are at liberty to go to bed—unless you prefer to join a party which has suddenly decided upon a moonlight bathing excursion.

Altogether, an idyllic existence, devoid of care. But perhaps the reader will now be able to realise why, after a fortnight of it, the ordinary healthy American may be excused for beginning to feel like a poodle chasing his own tail—especially in March, 1917, the moment at which our scene opens.

* * * * *

In those days America was full of Americans —even fuller than usual—for the simple reason that America was rated " neutral " in a World War, and her citizens were cooped up within their own borders.

Yet not quite all. Certain Americans, less diplomatic than their chosen rulers, had long since taken their own decision in the matter. Twenty-five thousand citizens of the United States were already serving, at the risk of forfeiting their own cherished citizenship, under various Allied flags. Hundreds more were driving ambulances behind the Allied lines. The Harvard Unit had taken over an entire British Base Hospital. Americans were rolling bandages and cutting surgical dressings for the Allies in every State in the Union. Americans were taking care of homeless women and children in France. Americans were fighting typhus in Serbia. Many an American business man was running his business with his left hand, reserving his right for the direction and endowment of Allied War Relief.

C*

Still, some odd hundred millions remained at
home. There were no Americans in the Ritz
at Paris, or in the Carlton at Cannes, or in
the Casino at Monte Carlo—these establishments
were devoted, for the most part, to sterner
uses—so Palm Beach, White Sulphur Springs,
French Lick and Pasadena were swamped by
a spring tide of pleasure-seekers. But pleasure,
when you come down to cases, is mainly the
resort of those who have failed in the pursuit
of happiness; and few of the pleasure-seekers
at Palm Beach in those days were entirely
happy. A sovereign people were standing aloof
from something which, whatever their heads
might say, their hearts told them was very
much their business.

Two years ago there really had been some
room for doubt on the matter. The Old World
had suddenly plunged into what, from a range
of three thousand ocean miles, looked like one of
the periodical scraps in which the monarchs
of Europe had indulged from the beginning of
time. The New World had shrugged its
shoulders and wondered how long presumably
enlightened nations would continue to tolerate
" the King business." Sides were taken to a
certain extent, but at first mainly for purposes
of academic debate. America as a whole
cherished a sentimental affection for France,

her ancient ally in her War of Independence.
New England, and ancient States like Virginia,
were mainly pro-British. On the opposite side
of the argument stood the Middle West, headed
by the great Germanic communities of
Wisconsin and Minnesota, solidly united and
suspiciously ready with words. To the Franco-
philes, for instance, who made play with
Lafayette's statue in Washington, these replied,
not altogether unreasonably, by pointing to
General Von Steuben standing in the opposite
corner of the same square. Short was the
ancestral friend, as well as Codlin.

Russia was a ticklish topic : the vast Jewish
community in the great cities saw to that. It
was well enough to extol Holy Russia and The
Little White Father as the heaven-sent pro-
tectors of small States like Serbia ; but how
could the greatest free Republic in the world
compound with its conscience to the extent of
toeing the line with the most corrupt and rotten
Despotism in Christendom ? Irish " exiles,"
too, most of whom had never seen Ireland
and none of whom had the slightest desire to
return there, were drawing subsidised com-
parisons between the British in Dublin and
the Germans in Brussels. Altogether it was
not surprising that Uncle Sam should have
demanded a little time to adjust his compasses

in the magnetic storm that raged about his head.

But now two years had elapsed. The greatest of all wars had branched out in directions undreamed of by the prophets ; and for the first time in history it had been made evident that if an international issue be vast enough all the world must take one side or the other in the end, or be ground up between the millstones. America was still officially at peace, but upon her soil—or rather beneath it—one of the bitterest, yet most romantic of campaigns was raging. Some day the history of that underground struggle in and for the heart of the United States will be written ; but the whole truth will never be told, for the simple reason that no one will believe it. It was a sheer battle of wits, inaudible and invisible, distinguished by no military pomp and entirely devoid of public acclamation. The participants therein were mainly men of the stamp which plays a game for its own sake, and sets the mark above the prize. All over America they were serving—as clerks, janitors, waiters, ships' stewards, what you will—taking notes, reporting symptoms and encouraging tendencies. Walls had ears—microphonic ears ; an incautiously spoken word in a hotel lounge might sink or save a liner in mid-Atlantic.

The written word was equally unsafe. A visitor to New York might return to his locked bedroom after an absence of five minutes to find the door still locked but his baggage ransacked and his papers rifled.

A new word had been coined, destined to wreck the German Empire and alter the face of the world for ever after—Propaganda. Its operations covered every field; nothing was too great or too small for it. A humorist in the British Intelligence Service became possessed of an ancient photograph of the German Ambassador to Washington disporting himself upon the beach at some watering-place with two damsels in distinctly arresting bathing-dresses. He sent it to a London society weekly, which published it in full page form; and in due course some hundred copies of the number containing the photograph evaded the submarines and arrived in New York. But—by three o'clock upon the afternoon of the second day, every single copy of that periodical had been mysteriously bought up and destroyed, while, such copies as had reached their destination direct had disappeared with equal celerity from club tables and hotel reading-rooms. It was only an affair of outposts, but each side distinguished itself.

But propaganda cuts deeper than that.

Below oceans of talk and streams of so-called literature, there were deeds. Wheat fields were fired in Kansas, that civilians might starve in Europe. In Connecticut munition factories were turning out shells for the Russian Army which the Russian Army was destined never to receive, because the Russian Munition Inspectors, being in the pay of the revolutionaries, who were in the pay of Germany, turned back consignment after consignment as below standard. In the North railway bridges were blown up, that Canadian soldiers might be held back from embarkation a few weeks longer. In the West a body paradoxically known as the International " Workers " of the World, inexplicably flush of cash, were calling upon Labour to labour no more until wars should cease. In the South negroes were being incited to the verge of a stampede by whispered suggestions of Equal Rights and a Black Republic.

Yet Palm Beach was crowded. But not with Germans, or for that matter pro-Germans. The sands were running out. Bernstorff, the German Ambassador, had received his passports, and had departed homeward in a Scandinavian liner, *faute de mieux*, six weeks previously. Things were beginning to be called by their right names. For some months certain devoted and sturdy exponents of Americanism had been submitting themselves to voluntary military training at the great camp of Plattsburg; these, after being reviled by the mob as Militarists of the deepest dye, were now being acclaimed by the same mouths as Apostles of Preparedness. The voice of the pro-German had died away in the land—to be heard no more until it should rise again, thinly disguised, as the voice of the peacemaker.

America's active participation in the War was merely a matter of time now. Uncle Sam, his long agony of uncertainty over, was out on his back porch, beating his ploughshare into a sword and prepared to go fighting mad at any moment.

CHAPTER VII   KHAKI FEVER
──

IT was high noon at Palm Beach, and a rolling chair, propelled by a coal-black gentleman in white raiment and containing an obvious Englishman in blue serge, was proceeding along a pleasant thoroughfare known as Sunset Avenue towards the sea.

The charioteer leaned forward confidentially and inquired :

" Do ah stop in at the Tilford home, Captain ? "

" You do, George."

" Ah suppose she will be all wait'n' on de po'ch," suggested George—" like yesterday, Captain ? "

George's surmise was correct. Mrs. Tilford *was* waiting—a very beautiful vision under a big tulle hat, through the wide brim of which the filtered sunshine irradiated a perfect oval face, a wide, sensitive, and a most attractive mouth, and a pair of appealing blue eyes. Altogether a woman, one would say, who required a man to lean upon. Truth to tell, there had never been any lack of applicants for this post, but Geraldine Tilford, a widow of more than three years' standing—ever since her twenty-second birthday, in fact—had so far kept the vacancy unfilled.

" Good morning, Captain Conway ! " she cried, with a smile which to another woman would have betrayed a certain lack of composure. " You didn't forget your promise, then ? "

" There are some promises," replied the gentleman addressed, handing her into the chair, " which are easier to keep than others. Bathing beach, George ! "

" Talking of promises," resumed Mrs. Tilford, as they bowled along in the pleasant intimacy of their conveyance, " have you forgotten the promise you made to me last night ? "

" Forgotten it ? It kept me awake till six o'clock this morning ! "

" But you'll keep it ? "

" Must I ? The idea terrifies me. I don't so much mind standing up and delivering a discourse to the Women's Uplift Guild at Clam Neck, Arkansaw—— "

" Don't you get fresh about our American place-names," Mrs. Tilford warned him playfully, " or I'll start right in with something about Marjoribanks, and Cholmondeley, and —Kirkcudbright ! "

Evidently the pair were on the best of terms. Dale Conway smiled disarmingly.

"Sorry! But you know what I mean. To hand out that line of talk to a Palm Beach audience—sophisticated, well-dined and slightly—— " He hesitated.

"'Lit up' is our current idiom," said his companion gently.

"Thank you!—'lit up'—in the ballroom at The Breakers—well, it calls for a degree of physical courage which I don't possess."

"Courage?" Mrs. Tilford's long eyelashes fluttered upward for a moment in a glance of genuine admiration. "Captain Conway, I know your record!"

"I shall begin to be sorry I ever told you that rotten story," said Conway, frowning. "I don't know why I did; I've never done such a thing to anyone before."

"That's why I prize it so. I know it makes you all wrought up and nervous having bouquets thrown at you; and I just love throwing them. But I promise not to do it any more in public, if you will let me do it occasionally in private. There!"

"Don't be silly, please!" replied Conway severely. "Now, let us get back to the lecture. You really want me to give it?"

"Yes—just to please me. Will you?"

For a moment Conway's eyes held Geraldine's with a boldness somewhat at variance with his recent expressions of diffidence.

" All right," he said, " I will."

Mrs. Tilford clapped her hands like a child.

" Oh, how lovely ! " she exclaimed. " You'll
let me pay the overhead expenses, won't you,
just as a little contribution to the cause we all
stand for ? I'll have them drape the platform
with the Allied flags—and the American flag
too, neutral or not ! I'll get old Mr. Storey
to preside ; he's about the most pro-British
thing on two legs around here ; and we'll charge
five dollars admission, and you shall send it all
to one of those perfectly wonderful War Relief
Funds of yours ; and I'll give just a tiny little
dinner-party for you first, and a little informal
supper after, and I'll invite—oh, it will be too
exciting ! "

And Geraldine Tilford, who, as the reader
will doubtless have gathered, was a lady of an
incurably romantic disposition, suffering in
addition from an acute attack of a malady
epidemic in those distant days but now
conspicuously extinct — Khaki Fever — laid
an impulsive little hand upon Conway's
sleeve.

Conway promptly covered the hand with his
own, as a skilful card-player covers a trick.

" How many people will be at the informal
supper ? " he asked.

" Well, let me see. My dinner-table only

holds twelve, but we needn't sit down. Twenty or thirty, maybe."

" Will you do me a favour ? "

" I'll say I will. What ? "

" Reduce the number."

" To how many ? "

Conway, bending his head closer, named a figure.

" Oh ! " said Geraldine, fluttered. " I shall have to think about that ! "

" To please me ? "

" Well, I'll see "—nervously. " Why, hallo, here we are at the bathing pavilion ! " She jumped out of the chair, obviously relieved at the respite. " I'll run in here and fix myself for the beach. That's the men's entrance, along by the steps. I'll meet you here in fifteen minutes."

She was as good as her word. A quarter of an hour later, a slim, piquant figure, sheathed from head to foot in a bathing creation of shimmering black silk, covered by a white wrap and set off by a head-band of many hues, she joined Conway, less ambitiously arrayed, at the rendezvous, and the pair picked their way down the crowded, babbling beach.

" Now I must tell you," Mrs. Tilford said, " about the people you are going to meet to-day."

Conway groaned.

"Another new bunch?"

"Yes. Don't forget you're a lion! I want to have you know everybody here. Old Mr. Storey is one. He's going to introduce you at your lecture, as I said; only he doesn't know it yet. Then there is his daughter Virginia—just about the cunningest thing that ever bobbed her hair; and her beau, Roger Marvin—he's crazy about her. Then Baby Studfield: I thought you'd like to meet one of our genuine sub-deb. types. Then Mrs. Wynne. She's a widow, but an older one than I am. She lives on Mount Vernon Street in Boston, but she doesn't allow that to make any difference. And then there's Colonel Winter. But of course you know him."

"I can't say I do. Should I?"

"Why, yes. He's in the British Army."

"Oh!" Conway nodded his head thoughtfully; then asked:

"Do you know his regiment?"

"No. Does it matter so much?"

"Yes, in one way. The British Army now contains about five million men, and I'm afraid I don't know half of them; so corroborative details are welcome. Moreover, I have run across so many British colonels in my lecturing travels over here who have never been nearer to the

Western Front than the Knickerbocker Bar, that
—well, one has to be careful, don't you know ! '

Mrs. Tilford laughed.

" That's a good one on you," she said.
" Colonel Winter is right out of your British
Embassy in Washington. He's a very, very
great friend of mine. He's some kind of dyed-
in-the-wool attaché there. I shall enjoy intro-
ducing you to one another. It's such fun seeing
two Englishmen meet for the first time : they're
just like a pair of strange dogs."

" British Embassy, eh ? " said Conway quickly.
" That's different."

" *Oh*, Gerr-*ee* ! "

Shrill cries assailed them from a neighbouring group, and a moment later Conway found
himself being presented, in the dexterous
American fashion, to a grey-haired lady with
a whimsical smile, who proved to be that Mrs.
Wynne who refused to be dazzled by the fact
that she resided in Mount Vernon Street,
Boston ; Mr. Storey, an old gentleman with a
fierce white moustache and the bearing of a
Kentucky colonel—as a matter of fact, he was
a bank president from New York—two
undeniably attractive young ladies whose combined ages must have fallen considerably short
of forty years ; a lithe, limber American boy
of about twenty-one, obviously bound hand

and foot to the chariot wheels of the blonder
young lady; and Colonel Winter, who proved
to be a middle-aged British officer, with a quiet
manner and a "tin arm"—the fruit of participation two and a half years ago in the Battle
of Le Cateau.

Having absorbed the new-comers, the party
settled down again upon the warm sand. Dale
Conway found himself sitting between Mrs.
Wynne and Geraldine Tilford. Opposite him,
under a large white umbrella, reclined Miss
Virginia Storey—the exponent of cunning and
bobbed hair.

"Well, Captain Conway," inquired that young
lady, with the engaging aplomb of youthful
America, "are you enjoying Palm Beach?"

Conway laughed.

"If I had a tail," he said, "I should wag it."

"Fine! And what strikes you as the most
attractive thing about the place?"

"You."

"I was hoping you'd say that," said Miss
Storey frankly; "only I was afraid you'd say
Gerry instead!"

"I meant all of you," explained Conway—
"especially in your present setting."

"You mean this sort of thing?" Virginia
indicated her bathing costume—a cherry-
coloured tunic, with glossy silk stockings and

sandals to match, set off by a black scarf about her fair hair, and a black sash.

" Yes. But do you mean to say that you go into the water in all that elaborate gear ? "

" Why, certainly. We'd get arrested if we didn't."

" You've got to remember, Captain Conway," said Mrs. Wynne, " that the Pilgrim Fathers were very austere old gentlemen. They established the tradition that it is indelicate to display the human skin to any considerable extent. That's why in these days American girls go bathing in silk stockings."

Conway chuckled.

" If you ask me, Mrs. Wynne," he replied, " I should say that the Pilgrim Fathers were neither so austere nor so old as they looked. There's nothing enhances an ankle like a silk stocking—and in the matter of ankles the rest of the world has to hand it to the American girl every time."

" This man," announced Baby Studfield to the world in general, " is the prize orchid-pinner. I adore him ! I know he's your beau, Gerry, dear, but I've got to say it."

Most Englishmen would have been embarrassed by this frank and public bestowal of a virgin affection ; but Conway merely laughed.

" The plaything of an hour," he said, shaking

his head; "that's all we are! In a few months your own countrymen will be in uniform, and Colonel Winter and I will be thrown aside like broken toys—broken tin soldiers! Eh, Colonel?"

Colonel Winter, thus addressed, murmured something non-committal, and reddened. This was the first time he had met Captain Conway in the flesh. He had heard rumours of him— of his success as a war-lecturer in the Middle West, of his charm of manner and winning personality. But Winter was a Regular soldier of the old breed, with certain very definite ideas upon the subject of good form and the correct attitude of an officer and a gentleman towards ladies; and this man, for all his charm and personality—and certainly he had both— struck him as a rather free and easy bounder. A bounder! Yes, that was why he disliked him so. The fact that Mrs. Tilford and Conway had arrived at the beach in the same chair for three mornings running had, of course, nothing to do with the case. The Colonel suspected that Mrs. Wynne shared his opinion; possibly old Storey, too.

But here he was wrong. For the moment Mr. Storey's patriotism outbalanced his sense of values.

"Uniform?" he cried. "You're right there, Captain Conway. This time next year Uncle

Sam will be holding up his head again, because there'll be a million of his uniforms in the trenches, with American boys inside them ! "

" That'll take quite a little responsibility off brother's shoulders," observed Virginia.

" *Your* brother ? " asked Conway.

" Yes. He's been serving in the Royal British Artillery quite a while. He had to take an oath of allegiance to King George to get in, too ! You'll admit that's going some for an American citizen ! "

" It's magnificent," said Conway. " You must be very proud of him."

" Well," interposed Miss Studfield stoutly, " I guess we shall be starting in with some Royal Artillery of our own soon—made up of nothing but little old brothers. It'll be a wonderful time ! "

" I wonder ! " said Mrs. Wynne, turning to Colonel Winter.

The Colonel nodded. He had seen the youth of another nation on fire for this very cause, and he knew the difference between anticipation and reality.

" Still," said Conway, skilfully diverting the conversation from its sombre trend—" promise that if America comes into the war you won't do one thing."

" What's that ? " asked several people.

" Send us lecturers. I know we deserve no mercy, after what we have done to you ; but promise ! "

" He's prospecting for an orchid for himself now," announced Baby Studfield.

" No ; I'm serious. Of course dull, respectable, semi-official bores like myself don't do any particular harm or good ; but this great land of yours is simply stiff with impostors and confidence men—most of them from London, I regret to say, though Canada has done her bit—exploiting the American national passion for information, however unreliable. I expect you have rounded up a few, Colonel, from the Embassy."

" Not many," replied Winter. " We have no authority. All we can do is to warn the American police, and even they can't act unless the man does something that brings him under the criminal code, which he is usually too smart to do. After all, why should he, when he can make all the money he wants by lecturing on a war about which no one can contradict him, even though he has never seen it ? "

" Never seen it ? " said Roger Marvin.

" No, not as a rule. Sheer bluff ! *Possunt quia posse videntur*, so to speak."

" I beg your pardon, Colonel," inquired Miss Studfield, with round eyes, " but *what* was that ? "

" A Latin tag ; I'm sorry ! "

" Freely translated," said Conway, coming gallantly and gratuitously to the rescue of his superior officer, " it means, Some People can Get Away with Murder."

" Oh ! Well, if you pull any more of that technical stuff on us poor defenceless women," replied Baby, " I warn you we shall leave you to it and go in swimming. But tell us some more about these confidence men. Did you ever meet any, Captain Conway ? "

" Lots."

" What are they like ? "

" Well, they varied a good deal. I particularly remember two. The first I came across in Chicago, at a vaudeville show—not in the Loop. He was attired in some kind of kilt, with a tin hat. Most of his front teeth were missing ; perhaps he had lost them in battle— perhaps not. He had a broken nose, too. He came on carrying an obsolete British rifle—a Martini-Henry, I think—with fixed bayonet, presented arms to the audience in a manner all his own, and told us of his experiences in the trenches. Most of his time there appeared to have been spent in exchanging repartees with his Divisional General ,in which our friend always scored heavily. He wound up by making a sort of rampart of furniture and climbing over it with the band playing, to show us how one stormed German trenches. I'm bound to say the audience ate it up. I got hold of him afterwards. He wasn't a bad fellow—a rolling stone from Clydebank, near Glasgow. He had been in America for more than twenty years— getting knocked about in the lowest walks of the entertainment profession—playing the fat policeman in the circus, the one who gets pushed into a tank or run over by a Ford, and so on. His chance had come to him suddenly with the war, and he had grabbed it. Having once been a private in a Scottish volunteer regiment, in the days of the old Saturday afternoon soldiers, he knew just enough of the jargon, when the demand came for wounded heroes, to get in on the ground floor. He was actually earning forty dollars a week. He knew it wouldn't last, but for the moment he was as happy as a sandboy. I must say I like people like that."

" He sounds lovely," said Baby Studfield.

" There's no denying," said Mr. Storey, " that crooks are usually most attractive people."

" They have to be," said Mrs. Wynne, " or there wouldn't be any use in their trying to be crooks. What was the other one like, Captain Conway?"

"He was a different customer altogether. I met him at Louisville—or, rather, I didn't meet him. He sent up his card to my room at the hotel and suggested that as we were both British officers in a strange land we might fore-gather for lunch. It was his card which roused my suspicions. It said : ' Captain Percy de Lacey. D.S.O.—British Army.' It didn't look right to me. ' British Army ' sounded rather an elastic term, and of course no officer with a D.S.O. would have D.S.O. printed on his card."

" And I never knew that ! " said Baby Studfield gravely.

" So I telephoned down to the hall, and asked him what his regiment was. He thought a little, and then said : ' The Sherwood Foresters.' After that I thought a little, and said I was in the Sherwood Foresters too, and would be pleased to meet a brother-officer. Of course, it was an error of the first magnitude. When I got downstairs my bird had flown, and I have never heard of him since."

" I have," said Colonel Winter unexpectedly.

" Oh, tell us ! " demanded a chorus of voices

" I attended his wedding."

" Well, what do you know about that ? " exclaimed Baby. " Where ? "

" In Buffalo. We had been on his track for some time, but we couldn't fasten anything definite on him until he committed the indis-cretion of getting engaged to a wealthy widow."

" I'm a widow, and not too badly off," remarked Mrs. Wynne calmly. " Where was the indiscretion ? "

" The indiscretion lay in his being married already. His lawful mate was a chorus girl in a Broadway show. She saw his photograph, and the widow's, in a Sunday paper ; and having been on the look-out for him for two years, was naturally gratified. She came to see us about it, and I went with her to Buffalo. There, with the assistance of the police, we separated Master Percy de Lacey from his prospective source of income at the eleventh hour. I don't quite know where he is now. I think he was deported to Canada, but he may be in Sing Sing."

" But how did your British Embassy get wise to this bird de Lacey in the first instance, Colonel ? " asked Roger Marvin.

" Oh, our Intelligence Service isn't so bad," said Winter briefly.

" You mean to say you keep tabs on all roving Britishers in the United States ? "

" We try to."

" Well, isn't that great ? I dare say you've even got a little pigeon-hole in Washington for Captain Conway here."

" I shouldn't wonder."

" As a matter of fact," said Conway, " I'm not so sure. I know I ought to have reported formally at Washington long ago, Colonel; but I've never done it, for the simple reason that I've never been there yet. I came into the country by Canada. I had been invalided out of the army after the spring attack at Ypres, nearly two years ago——"

" Were you badly wounded Captain Conway ? " asked Virginia sympathetically.

" I wasn't exactly wounded——"

" He was very badly gassed," interposed Geraldine Tilford, with all the pomp of one imparting exclusive information. " He was given special leave by the British War Office to come over here for a while and have his lungs attended to. Isn't that so, Captain Conway ? "

" Yes ; by two wonderful American specialists —brothers, Mayo by name—in Detroit."

" Rochester," corrected Mr. Storey.

" I beg your pardon ; it was Rochester."

" And is. They are a famous pair there."

" They are a wonderful pair. Their treatment was so successful that after a few months I was tempted to try a little public speaking on behalf of the Allies. Something of the kind was very badly wanted in the Middle West at the time ; and before I knew where I was I had fallen for a lecture tour, and found myself booked solid for six months. I began to feel the strain badly at last, so I came here for a few weeks' vacation. And that," concluded Conway with his quick, attractive smile, " is the whole sad tale of how I came to be what I am—a soap-box orator."

" Captain Conway, you must not belittle yourself ! " exclaimed Mr. Storey characteristically. " I am told you are a born speaker."

Conway laughed composedly.

" A Spellbinder from Way Back—eh, sir ? No, I'm pretty awful, really. Still, one may do a bit of good here and there—besides helping one's pet war charities."

Suddenly Geraldine Tilford sat up. She had taken little part in the conversation, but now the time had come for her to play her master card.

" You will all have a chance to know for yourselves in a few days how Captain Conway speaks," she announced triumphantly ; " because he is going to lecture right here in Palm Beach ! "

And forthwith she plunged into the details of the contemplated function. Within ten minutes Mr. Storey had accepted the post of chairman, Roger Marvin had undertaken to arrange for the necessary publicity, and the young ladies present, having appointed themselves Principal Usherettes, were feverishly attacking the problem of a costume, or possibly uniform, which should be at once becoming, stunning, and symbolical

D

of the approaching union of hearts between
English-speaking races, when a general upheaval
all over the beach announced that cocktail time
was approaching, and that if they were going to
bathe they would have to proceed from words to
deeds forthwith. Next moment everyone was
scampering down to the water, with the exception
of Mr. Storey, Mrs. Wynne, and the incapacitated
Winter.

" That's a fine type of British soldier, Colonel,"
said Mr. Storey warmly. " What personality!
Did you see how those young folks hung on his
words ? "

" I guess Geraldine Tilford would have preferred to hang around his neck," commented
Mrs. Wynne. " Well, she saw him first, I'll
allow."

Colonel Winter said nothing. He was an honest
person, and he could not express admiration
that he did not feel. Besides, he was wondering
why a man who had spent several months under-
going medical treatment in the city of Rochester
should have referred to that city as Detroit.

I

DALE CONWAY paused and glanced at his wrist-watch. In England men wear wrist-watches as a matter of masculine custom, and despise watch-chains as effeminate : in America the converse holds good. A wrist-watch upon an American man is—or was in those days—a target for rugged mirth. But the audience in The Breakers Ballroom gave no sign. The Spellbinder from Way Back had justified his own jesting description of himself.

He looked up again, and smiled disarmingly.

" Ladies and gentlemen," he said, " I observe that I have bored you for nearly an hour. This must stop. I must stop ! "

There was dissent here—quite sincere dissent.

" But I must say one word more. It is this. I am profoundly moved by the manner in wh'ch you have helped me along to-night ; and I want to say so. An Englishman can never say ' thank you ! ' prettily, and he knows it ; so sometimes he omits the formality altogether. Please

99

remember that fact next time an Englishman treats you abruptly; remember that he is dying to make a pretty speech, but can't. For my part, I will content myself by saying the bare words, in the sure and certain belief that you will read into them the genuine emotion that lies at the back of them." Conway's voice shook a little.

There was a sympathetic stir throughout the room. Geraldine Tilford, ecstatic behind a potted palm, dabbed her eyes.

" I have kept my tale," continued Conway in a steadier voice, " as simple as possible, because I know that simple truth is what you want at a time like this. I have avoided technicalities; I have avoided politics; and in particular I have avoided anything in the shape of partisan statement, because I am well aware that I stand upon neutral soil, addressing a strictly neutral audience ! "

There was a ripple of laughter. Here at last was an Englishman with a sense of humour.

" So I have confined my discourse to a simple theme that lies very near my own heart—the theme of that very effectually disguised knight-errant, Thomas Atkins. That is why I have labelled my lecture ' Human Nature at the Front '—because Tommy is the most human person that I know. I have tried to depict for

you his experiences during an average round of
twenty-four hours in the trenches. Perhaps I
have toned down the horrors a little, and
exaggerated the humour ; but to an American
audience—the quickest audience in the world,
by the way—it is sufficient to indicate without
elaborating. The British Tommy, especially the
old regular, is an inarticulate person ; he
would be embarrassed to the point of profanity
if he knew we were talking about him now ;
but—well, he has saved England ; and England
means a good deal to some of us here present."

The applause broke forth again.

" What he has done will probably never be
known to the world, because to a great extent
the memory of his achievements will be obscured
and overlaid by greater achievements still to
come—the achievements, for the most part, of
other people. What people, I need not specify.
But "—for the first time the speaker's voice
rose above conversational level, and his hands
were stretched towards his audience in a
gesture of entreaty—" I want to make a little
appeal to you. When the great day comes, when
the miracle of peace is vouchsafed to us again, and
the glory and the praise are duly bestowed, as
they always must be, upon those who are in at
the finish I ask that you will pay in your hearts
some small tribute of remembrance to those

vanished legions of nameless men who stood up
to the first rush, and by their sacrifice paved
the way for your victory."

Conway's hands fell to his sides again, and he
sank, like a man suddenly weary, into his chair
behind the flag-draped table. There were tears
in his eyes.

Next moment the audience were on their feet,
cheering, waving, weeping. When the most
impulsive and the warmest-hearted nation in
the world is touched to the quick, it is not
ashamed to say so. It was five minutes at
least before Mr. Storey, the chairman, was able
to obtain a hearing. That youthful septuage-
narian had plainly reached the point at which he
had to make a speech or suffer serious internal
injury. He had introduced Conway to his
audience with commendable brevity. Now his
moment had come.   He rose to his feet.

" In England," he began, " they have a
custom, after a speaker has spoken his piece,
of awarding him a vote of thanks—but only in
the accepted British fashion. That is to say,
the motion is first proposed and seconded,
usually at some length ; after that it is put to
the meeting, and if anyone present feels like
opposing it he is perfectly at liberty to do so.
Finally, along towards bedtime, the proposal is
confirmed by the audience, and the speaker goes

home happy in the knowledge that, whatever has been awarded to him, nothing short of an Amendment to the British Constitution can take it away from him ! "

There was a general laugh of appreciation of this exactly right note. Conway led it.

" But I should hate," continued the old gentleman, " to be responsible for instituting any procedure of that kind here to-night. In fact, it would be impossible. We are a young nation, and an impulsive nation, and a susceptible nation ; and when a man gets us right where our hearts live, as Captain Conway has got us to-night—well, there is only one thing to do, and that is to award him the vote of thanks first and propose it afterwards."

The company promptly took the speaker at his word, and the vote of thanks was awarded for some minutes. John Storey turned to Conway.

" You hear that, Captain Conway ? " he said. " It is yours—all yours—and you deserve every bit of it, and more. I am not going to spoil it by adding any verbal embroidery." He turned to the audience again. " But before I sit down," he said, " I desire in particular to thank Captain Conway for two things. In the first place he has not told us to get into the game ; and in the second he hasn't talked about himself. We all know here that we *ought* to be in the game—— "

There was another great shout.

" ——and we should not have resented it if Captain Conway *had* told us so—coming from him, of course. Also, we should have been intensely interested to hear some of the Captain's own personal experiences in the War. But he did not give them to us. On the whole I'm glad, in both cases. If he had given us fireworks, we should no doubt have enjoyed them ; but what he gave us was the quiet restraint and curiously effective understatement of an English gentleman ; and that was what we were looking for. In our hearts we Americans cherish a picture of the ideal soldier—the man who is both modest and brave. Such men have been fighting our battles for us over there for more than two years. But now "—the old man's voice rang out exultantly—" we are going to reinforce them—reinforce them with men of like pattern to themselves—men speaking the same language— men burning to make up for lost time and lift some of that intolerable burden from the shoulders which have borne the whole of it too long. It has not been altogether our fault. We have been kept out of things for at least a year by a pure accident of the calendar—the Presidential Election of last November. It had to come, but it came at an unfortunate time. But now it is over, thank God!"—another shout went up—"and our country is once more being led by a leader and not by a candidate for office." He turned suddenly, and laid an impulsive hand upon Conway's shoulder. "Captain Conway, if you listen carefully, you will hear the tramp of armed thousands beginning to vibrate upon our soil. To-day they are still a long way behind you; but to-morrow they will be shoulder to shoulder with you; and presently, if I know the spirit of the American boy, all you will be able to see will be a small cloud of dust upon the horizon in front of you! God bless you, and God bless all of us!"

And the old man sat down—spent, radiant, and entirely happy for the first time since the invasion of Belgium.

2

There was no mistaking the impression that Conway had created. As the audience dispersed to the further preoccupations of the evening— roulette, dancing, supper, or bed—there was but one opinion. The lecture had contained nothing strikingly new nor in the least sensational, as sensations went in those hectic days; but its modest delivery and its tactful consideration of American susceptibilities—and

D*

America, being the youngest, is the most sensitive country in the world—combined with the lecturer's own attractive personality, had struck deep. Orchids, as Miss Studfield would have said, were the order of the day.

"That's a type of man, Colonel," announced Mr. Storey, still aglow, "that only England can produce. Don't you agree, Mrs. Wynne?"

"Well, I'm not so sure," said Mrs. Wynne, with her lazy smile. "I'll admit he's a clever man. He knows our national weaknesses, and he tickles us just where we like to be tickled. But I wouldn't call that a universal British characteristic. Would you, Colonel Winter?"

"Five years in the diplomatic society of Washington has convinced me of the mournful truth of your words, Mrs. Wynne," said Winter. "Still, I thought Conway made an admirable speech."

"As soon as I get back to New York," said Mr. Storey, "I'm going to take Carnegie Hall for him; and if I can fix things all right, it will be a turnaway. Will you be there, Colonel?"

"We'll send somebody from the Embassy, be sure," said Winter. "Good-night, and good-bye. My leave is over, and I'm off to Washington by the night train."

"When you get there," said Mr. Storey, as

he shook hands, " oblige me by putting a bullet into—— "

He mentioned the name of a prominent native politician, notorious for pacifism of a windy and tearful brand, and departed reverberatingly, in search of Mrs. Wynne's rolling chair. Winter, after a not very hopeful survey of the immediate landscape, walked off by himself in the soft moonlight, rather forlornly.

He was a bachelor, though not from choice. In love he was a better stayer than starter, and once before in his life in India he had been forestalled by a readier opponent. He had realised during the past fortnight that history was about to repeat herself, in Palm Beach. Hence the night train to Washington. Still, he was a just man.

" Damned good propaganda," he said to himself—" damned good, whoever the fellow is ! I liked him better to-night. There were moments when he seemed absolutely *pukka*. He's certainly more convincing on a platform than in a drawing-room : the hairy heel is less conspicuous at that range. Still, I'd like to see his balance sheet, curse him ! "

Outside The Breakers, Baby Studfield, still clad in her Usherette costume—a grossly irregular but quite attractive feminisation of the uniform of His Majesty's Brigade of Guards—was about to climb into the chair of a young gentleman friend, one Barry Gates by name, who had been waiting for her for more than two hours, when she espied Conway and Mrs. Tilford emerging from the brightly illuminated entrance of the hotel. Deserting her long-suffering cavalier, Baby ran to the foot of the steps.

"That was a perfectly wonderful talk you gave us, Captain Conway," she said; "and you made me cry, if that's any satisfaction. Still, I want to tell you something. We love your Tommies, and they are great; but you wait about six months, and then see what this little old country of ours can do."

"That's the first really sensible remark I've heard this evening," said Conway, shaking hands. "Good night, Miss America—and good luck!" He kissed the flushed child's hand, and she ran back to her escort, with swelling heart.

"If you dare to speak to me for the next five minutes, Barry," she said as she climbed into the chair, "I'll kill you!"

"Just as you say, Baby," replied the docile Mr. Gates.

They trundled silently away into the moonlight. Conway whistled up the patient George from his moorings in the shadow of a neighbouring palm.

" Do we all go to the Tilford Home, Captain ? " inquired George, as Conway took his seat beside his hostess.

" We do, George."

" Right away, suh ! "

The last couple to leave were Virginia Storey and Roger Marvin.

" Virginia, will you come around to the Poinciana and dance ? " said the boy.

" No, Roger, thank you : I'm kind of all in to-night. You can walk along with me, if you like ; we won't have a chair."

Together they set off in the moonlight, arms linked. American boys and girls are much less self-conscious than ours. They develop more rapidly ; indeed, they develop one another. The monastic system which segregates our adolescents is unknown in America. The American boy is curiously at home in the company of the opposite sex, because he is seldom out of it. He spends all his boyhood in his home ; and he is educated, in most cases, at a day school, which he attends with his sister—and other boys' sisters. Consequently he is never independent of female society—as we sometimes think we are—and when he is about twenty-one or so he marries the girl from next door, and there is an end of it—or the beginning.

Roger Marvin was twenty-one. Virginia was

eighteen, and her father's daughter. To-night
she was in an ecstatic mood, which in a woman
very often means a melting mood. Young
America's love of country is a curiously passionate
thing: there is still a touch of the Declaration
of Independence about it. To-night, in her eager
young heart, Virginia could hear, like her father,
the tramp of the thousands who were coming to
vindicate America's fighting qualities and
America's honour in the eyes of the world.
And the boy at her side would be among those
thousands—among the very first of them! Her
arm stiffened suddenly within his, half proudly,
half-fearfully.

The ever-watchful Roger, deciding very
sensibly, to take a chance, responded by sliding
his hand respectfully into hers. She laughed,
shakily, and looked away, but did not withdraw
her hand.

Presently they were conscious of a house
among the palms close by—Geraldine Tilford's
house. Lights were burning in the dining-
room.

"Geraldine's having a supper party," said
Virginia, chiefly for the sake of saying something.

"Supper for two, I'll tell the world!" commented Roger.

They walked on a little farther.

" I guess Geraldine can land her fish any time she wants now," continued Virginia, still making conversation.

" It shouldn't be difficult. Geraldine's some bait, with her face and her bank roll. I should worry about being that fish ! "

" Do you admire Geraldine so much ? " inquired Virginia, looking up swiftly.

It was what is known as a leading and provocative question, and it brought that simmering caldron, Master Roger Marvin, to boiling point. Impulsively he halted in the middle of the moon-dappled road, and took the girl's hand in his.

" Virginia," he whispered, " you know I admire no one in the world but you ; and—and—I love you—and I always have—and I want you to marry me, right now—before we get into this war. Will you ? " His arms went round her slim young body.

Virginia smiled up at him, largely.

" I'll say I will, my dear," she replied ; and her eyes were wet.

Let us leave them to themselves. Neither of them will ever have a moment quite like this again in all their lives ; and who are we to intrude upon them ? Let us retrace our steps to a more sophisticated quarter.

3

" This," said Dale Conway, leaning back in his chair and exhaling a blue cloud from one of Mrs. Tilford's cigars, " is bliss ! " He leaned forward again. " Geraldine ! "

His hostess, sitting on the other side of the table, quivered. Her incurably romantic little heart began to bump. The late lamented Joshua Tilford had never awakened thrills of this kind in her by the mere utterance of her Christian name. He had been a good, sound man of business, an utterly prosaic person from a small town in Illinois—an undoubted success on Wall Street, but a complete failure on Riverside Drive. His instincts were entirely commercial and domestic ; and though Geraldine had striven hard to inject romance into him, he had disappointed her. In fact, he had died under the operation.

After his demise Geraldine, now in her twenty-third year, decided that she had done her duty by the prose of this world, and was entitled at last to her share of its poetry—a decision which had considerably narrowed her field in the selection of a second husband. Troubadours are scarce in American society— indeed, in all modern society, which is affected with an exaggerated sense of humour—and for

two years Geraldine had wearily rejected the
advances of a stream of lawyers, politicians,
stockbrokers, and needy persons frankly in
search of a permanent meal-ticket. After
making the acquaintance of Colonel Winter in
Washington six months previously, she had
been conscious of a leaning towards a husband
in uniform. Then, ten days ago, she had met
Dale Conway—soldier, poet, and spellbinder—
and had recognised her affinity almost immediately. And now, as Dale Conway leaned across
the table and said " Geraldine ! " she realised
that her affinity had recognised her.

The affinity was gazing at her, with glowing
eyes.

" Do you mind my calling you Geraldine ?"
he asked.

" Why, no."

" Thank you ! " He came a little closer.
" Shall I tell you what you are ? "

" Yes, if you like. What am I ? "

" An oasis."

" You mean—a thing in a desert ? "

" Yes—a human oasis. Something very rare,
and soothing, and refreshing——"

" O-o-oh ! "—in a rapturous whisper. Joshua
had never said things like this.

" ——that a traveller, if he is lucky, may
encounter once or twice in his journey through

—the wilderness." Conway paused, and took up his cigar again.

" Has your journey taken you through the wilderness ? " asked Geraldine, with a sudden soft glance.

Conway nodded.

" I suppose it has, most of the time. I'm not squealing. I'm a philosopher. It's mainly a matter of luck, and how you begin."

" How true that is," said Geraldine with a sigh.

" Yes, every time. Sometimes, early in life, before we are able to see very clearly ahead, and when we are young and impulsive, we take a step which carries us off the green path and points us straight for the wilderness. And before we know where we are "—Conway shook his head regretfully—" we find ourselves right in the middle of it. And some of us never get back."

" I know," said Geraldine. She looked up, as to a confessor. " I—I made a step like that once."

" You mean—your marriage ? "

" Yes."

" Was he unkind to you ? Did he ill-treat you ? " Conway's voice suddenly hardened. He had a fierce hatred of anything like physical cruelty.

"Oh, no. He was the gentlest thing. But —well, you know how it goes. I guess his *aura* was wrong for me."

Conway nodded sympathetically.

"Love is everything," he said. "If it's not there, nothing else will do." He sighed deeply.

Presently Geraldine inquired timidly:

"Would you think me terribly curious if I asked you what was your false step?"

Again Conway smiled.

"I have made more than one, I'm afraid," he said; "but the one we are thinking of was —the same as yours."

"You married?"

"Yes."

"The wrong woman?"

"Yes. No—that's not fair! Perhaps I should say she married the wrong man."

"How chivalrous you are! But do you mean to tell me she didn't love you?"

"She didn't understand me. (That's a bromide, I know; but a truth doesn't cease to be a truth because it has become bromidic.) Somehow I never could get much response out of her. Perhaps it was my fault; too rough a diamond, and so forth. I haven't seen her for nearly fifteen years. I expect she has been happily married to someone else this long while."

"Was she beautiful?"

" Very—in a cold-storage sort of way. But she must be getting on now : nearly forty, I should say."

Geraldine was suddenly conscious of a kinder feeling towards the former Mrs. Conway.

" And you," she said softly, " are all alone ? "

" Yes."

" And when you go home after the war, you'll have no home to go to ? "

" No." He laughed bitterly. " Home is a word that means nothing to me. I've been a wanderer, a rolling stone, all my life. This war was a godsend to me, in a sense. It took me away from—myself."

" You poor man ! Fancy welcoming a war ! But—perhaps you will stay right here in America ? "

" Do you think America wants me ? "

Here was a question precisely similar to that recently propounded to Roger Marvin by Virginia Storey ; and it had the same effect. Geraldine's heart was suddenly filled by a wave of real pity and affection.

" I think I know one person who does," she said.

Their eyes met across the table. Dale Conway rose from his seat and knelt upon the floor by Geraldine's chair. His sang-froid had left him : he was breathless and agitated. There was a look in his face of a strong swimmer in deep waters, suddenly conscious of an unbelievable foothold.

" Do you really mean that ? " he whispered. " You beautiful thing ! You really care ? "

Geraldine bowed her golden head.

" You could love a broken man—a piece of driftwood—like me ? " Conway's forehead was resting on her arm now. For a moment he really was a broken man, really a piece of drift-wood.

Geraldine lay a fluttering hand upon his head.

" You'll marry me ? " he murmured.

" Whenever you say, Dale, dear."

* * * * *

They bade one another good night on the veranda a few minutes later.

" I'll call for you to-morrow morning, and we'll go down to the beach for our usual wash and brush up—eh ? " suggested Conway. He was his easy-going self again now.

" We certainly will," said Geraldine enthusiastically. " And we'll tell *everybody* ! "

Conway cleared his throat.

" Well—do you know—don't think me infernally romantic, dear—but wouldn't it be rather jolly to keep it to our two selves for a bit—just to be our secret, and no one else's ? "

Geraldine looked up, in genuine concern. The corners of her mouth were drooping.

"Why, Dale, I'm so proud of you. I want to—— "

"But think what it all means—the publicity—the interviews—our photographs in the Sunday papers, and—er—so on. Can't I have you all to myself just for a while—till we get back to New York, perhaps? That'll give us time to make all our wedding arrangements in peace. Then, when we're ready—*quite* ready—we'll announce our engagement and get married directly after—say, in a fortnight, or a week During that time I promise you shall take me to every pink tea in sight and pass me round to your heart's content. Will that satisfy you? "

Geraldine buried her face in his shoulder.

"Anything satisfies me that satisfies you, honey," she murmured.

A supplementary good night followed.

"This time," Geraldine whispered, with her arms about his neck, "I hope you are going to get the wife you deserve."

Conway laughed lightly.

"I hope not! " he said.

ON April 2nd, 1917, the United States declared war upon Germany, and the cork was out of the bottle at last. Altogether a fine effervescent moment.

Conscription was passed by acclamation—there was no sentimental time-wasting over the Voluntary System in this case—and within a few weeks some twelve million able-bodied young Americans had registered for service. For the moment they could do no more. They had no arms or equipment : as in England, the peace-at-any-price party had seen to that. Neither was there any machinery in existence for housing, feeding, clothing, or doctoring them. But the mere fact that some of the finest human material in the world was destined to die of exposure and preventable sickness within its own borders during the next twelve months in order to vindicate the glorious doctrine of Unpreparedness and acquit certain virtuous non-combatants of all suspicion of having planned a brutal war of conquest was, as usual, lost to view in a tumult of popular enthusiasm. Uncle Sam's hat was in the ring at last, and for the moment that was all that mattered.

Khaki fever—or rather olive-drab fever—ran high. The humblest doughboy in the newest of uniforms was, quite rightly, a hero, and was expected to comport himself as such : at any moment he must be ready, held shoulder-high by a street crowd, to make a recruiting speech or expound the military situation " over there." A person in " civvies," on the other hand, was an object of suspicion. Later it became necessary to provide every man engaged upon legitimate civilian work with a certificate of exemption, to be shown to any patriotically disposed mob which might desire to examine his credentials as a preliminary to lynching him for a spy or man-handling him for a shirker.

The sinews of war were not forgotten. A vast Loan was raised, not according to the high and hidden mysteries of banking and under-writing, but by direct appeal to the people. War Bonds were on sale everywhere—by girls in fancy dress, by hotel clerks, by policemen on point duty ; across the counters of drug stores, at smoking concerts, and between the acts at theatres, where the principals of the company officiated as auctioneers. The American citizen was charged to buy a Liberty Bond for the

baby, and he bought one. He was commanded
to give until it hurt, and he gave. Never was
there a more spontaneous outpouring of the
natural spirit of a generous people.

But behind the tumult and the shouting
practical men were getting to work. Great
training camps sprang up in every State.
Invitations were sent to France and Britain for
military instructors who could bring to the
American people the latest and grimmest lessons
of actual warfare. Political Missions began to
arrive from Allied countries, and vast crowds
on Fifth Avenue were agreeably occupied for
some weeks in cheering to the echo embarrassed
foreign statesmen in top hats, accompanied by
inarticulate Field-Marshals almost too dazed to
speak their own language and quite incapable
of understanding any other.

The propaganda battle entered upon a new
and exciting phase. The long-drawn, unofficial,
underground struggle between the emissaries
of Britain and Germany came to a dramatic
conclusion ; for the American police authorities,
having abandoned their benevolent impartiality,
could now with propriety make use of a painfully
acquired dossier, supplied by their new colleagues,
of the multifold ramifications of the German spy
system. The principal Teutonic agents were
rounded up in a few days, and the law of the land,

having dealt faithfully with these, set out with cheery gusto to hunt for more.

Allied officers already in America became social pearls of great price, to their extreme discomfort. They were invited—nay bidden— to wear uniform at all times, partly for the advertisement of the common cause, partly for their own protection in a land suffering from the first violent convulsions of spy-mania. Consequently a large number of retiring Britons, who feared no foe but hated being made conspicuous, were compelled to emerge from the comfortable security of mufti and expose themselves in full war-paint to the affectionate plaudits of a public to whom such exhibitions were an entire novelty—an experience fraught with special embarrassment for Brigadier-Generals in brass hats and the representatives of the kilted regiments.

Permission was readily granted to the Allies to seek recruits among their own compatriots settled upon American soil; and when the inevitable difficulties connected with wives and children and separation allowances had been adjusted to a scale commensurate with American standards of living, some thirty thousand expatriated Britons duly returned to Europe to fight for the flag under which they had been born. All this involved considerable pother, for you cannot conduct recruiting agencies without attestations, and swearing in, and medical examination.

One night in New York Colonel Winter, who had come from Washington on matters connected with this very business, dined at the Ritz with an old friend and comrade-in-arms, one Jimmy Blackadder, who had landed in New York that morning upon the staff of yet another British Mission.

" This is a bit of a change from our last meal together, Tom—what ! " remarked Blackadder, sitting down contentedly and unfolding his napkin.

" Let me see—where was that ? "

" In the *Trois Amis*, at Ouderdom."

" Of course. I remember now—back at rest from Hooge. What an unexpected little haven that pub was, in that ocean of mud! And the meals Madame managed to provide for us ! "

" Yes ; and that mysterious little store of Clicquot of hers ! " Jimmy Blackadder smacked his lips, for he loved the flesh-pots. " By the way, what are we going to drink to-night ? "

" Sorry, old man, but we are going to drink some nice ice-water."

" God preserve us ! Why ? Have you turned teetotaller in your old age, or has Prohibition come at last ? "

" Neither—as yet. But the powers that be

over here—or rather the powers behind the powers that be—have just signified their appreciation of the patriotism and trustworthiness of the men who are going to fight for them by restricting the privilege of alcoholic refreshment to those who are not. No American soldier in uniform is allowed to come within twenty yards of a drink."

" Officers included ? "

" Officers included. We British have therefore agreed among ourselves not to add to the sufferings of our esteemed colleagues by drinking in their presence, that's all. I'll give you a spot of something upstairs later on."

" It reminds me," remarked Blackadder, ruefully sipping his ice-water, " of that time when we came back to Ouderdom from a week's trenches with our tongues hanging right out, to find that the *Trois Amis* had been closed up tight for a fortnight by the Town Major of Renninghelst, because Madame had been caught selling brandy to the Tommies. She reopened the day after we went back to the line. Do you remember ? "

" Do I not ? How we cursed that same Town Major ! Still, I suppose he was doing his duty. I've been conscious lately of a distinctly softer feeling towards Town Majors and other censors of military morals."

" Why ? "

" I've just been made one myself."

" Don't tell me you're Town Major of New York ! "

" No ; but I'm an Assistant Provost Marshal, for the time being. There are so many odd British Missions and details, not to mention individuals, knocking about all over this big country just now that it is time they were brought under some kind of supervision. It is to be my pleasant task to sort out the sheep from the goats."

" Goats ? "

" Yes—crooks."

" You mean, some of our fellows over here are wrong 'uns ? " inquired that simple soldier, Jimmy Blackadder.

" Out and outers—though, mind you, most of them aren't soldiers at all, but military impersonators—of varying skill. Half the swell mobsmen of the West End of London have been over here for two years, posing as wounded heroes or secret service men. There are one or two real artists at the job, I will admit. Some of them have had a royal time of it."

" Couldn't your Embassy people have put them in clink—on suspicion, or something ? "

" You can't put people in clink, on suspicion, or anything else, when they are living under the protection of somebody else's flag, my lad. But

now, with all our flags pooled, so to speak, we
have a legal footing over here, and I intend to
get busy with the drag-net."

"Well, I suppose it takes all sorts to make a
war," remarked Jimmy Blackadder tolerantly.
"An army too, for that matter. I remember
a queer case out in Belgium a year or two ago.
I was on a Corps Staff by that time, and chance
brought me into official contact with one of the
most plausible liars I have ever met."

"Not a member of the Staff?"

"Oh, no; just an afternoon caller. He was a
Field Cashier."

"What's that? Something new since my
day."

"An Army Pay Corps *wallah*—a capitalist
who dashes about in a car between the Base
and the Line carrying untold sums of money,
chiefly in ten franc notes, to pay the troops.
They used to cash cheques on Cox's, too, and
chance it. I tell you, a very present help in
trouble!"

"What about this customer?"

"He came buzzing into that very place we
were talking of just now, Outerdom, one wet
afternoon in October, from the direction of
Canada Huts—that was a Rest Camp on a mud-
flat just off the Dickebusch Road—and pulled
up his car outside the old *Trois Amis*, all of a

doodah, and asked the sentry where Corps
Headquarters was. The sentry told him, and
he came right in to where we were sitting, and
reported to the General direct. He was a new
General, just out from home, and he hadn't
quite shaken off the Whitehall manner of doing
things. He sent for pens and ink and somebody
to take shorthand notes, and made a regular
tamasha. Apparently our friend in the car had
had a narrow escape. He had been driving up
to the Line from Hazebrouck, loaded up to the
hatches with money—the pay of a Division, in
fact—and had run right into a bombardment
which was going on somewhere near Hellblast
Corner. (Of course he had no right to be there
at all ; the place was a recognised danger spot
and the road had been out of bounds for months ;
but our new General didn't know that.) Our
Field Cashier, considering it his duty to press on
to victory at all costs, had shoved down his
accelerator and made a dash for it. He got
through, but in the excitement of the moment
omitted to observe that the big leather wallet
on the seat beside him, containing his cargo, had
flapped open, and that most of the money had
blown away. Having at last noted his adverse
balance, he had come along to report, with a
view to having a search party detailed and his
personal honour vindicated. He was terribly

gentlemanly about it all ; courted a full inquiry, and so on."

" What did he look like ? A counter-jumper ? "

" No : he looked like a soldier. That was the funny thing about it. He had a South African ribbon up, too. Still, there was something about him—you know ! Something not *quite !* "

" I know. What did the Corps Commander do about it ? "

" He asked our sportsman if he had been alone in the car, and if so, why ? "

" That was rather a facer. What was the answer ? "

" It was all ready. His chauffeur had suddenly reported sick at Hazebrouck ; but, rather than fail in his duty and deprive us poor fellows of our pocket money, he had decided to drive the Ford himself."

" He seems to have been the slave of duty. What happened next ? "

" None of us really suspected him : we merely regarded him as a bit of a *bukh*-stick from Threadneedle Street. But the General told him that in the absence of any corroborative evidence of his statement, and as a matter of form, he had better consider himself under arrest for the time being. Then he rang up some gun-pits near Hellblast Corner, and asked them if they had been shelled that afternoon, and if so, at what hour. They replied, very respectfully, that Hellblast Corner had been punctually shelled every ten minutes, night and day, for the last eighteen months ; and what other damn silly question could they have the pleasure of answering ?—or words to that effect. That rather flummoxed the General, so he switched off from the Line and rang up Hazebrouck, to ask if they had mislaid a Field Cashier. Unfortunately, the number was engaged : somebody's Strength Return or Weather Report was going through. So the General told our guest to sit round and wait for further instructions. After that, we forgot all about him for a couple of hours. The next thing we knew was that he was gone."

" Bolted ? "

" Yes. It was dark by this time, and as no officer had been detailed to look after him, and none of the men had any authority to stop him, he simply strolled into the street, got his car, and drove off."

" To Hazebrouck ? "

" Not so as you'd notice it. He disappeared into the blue. The car was found weeks later at Havre, so presumably he took ship from there. After all, a man with the pay of a Division in his possession, in convenient currency,

E

ought to be able to fix up a little matter like
that. Anyhow, he was never heard of again.
Personally, I rather liked what I remember of
him ; he was a cheerful knave ! "

"He sounds like a real artist," said Tom
Winter. "What was his name ? "

"Cranford. No, wait a minute ! Canfield—
no—Cradock ! That was it—Captain Denis
Cradock. I remember he was rather particular
about the Denis. Made quite a fuss when the
note-taking person spelt it with two n's."
Jimmy Blackadder pushed back his chair.
"Now what about the little spot of something
upstairs ? Are you ready ? "

"Right ! Wait till I get the bill. Check,
please, waiter ! "

An obsequious alien hurried off to the pay-
desk, and the two officers sat waiting, surveying
the animated scene about them.

"Fair women and brave men—what ? "
remarked Blackadder, in a sudden outburst
of sentimentality. "They're a likely looking
crowd, Tom."

"Who ; the men or the women ? "

"The women go without saying : I see I am
booked for heart trouble over here. By the
way, old chap, have you escaped ? "

"Quite, thanks." Tom Winter was strangely
emphatic.

"Good. But I was speaking of the men for the moment. I wouldn't mind commanding a brigade of them. It's rum to see so many privates feeding in a place like this, though— and a couple of naval ratings, too. What pay do they get, for goodness' sake?"

"They don't need to worry about their pay. These lads mostly live in marble mansions on Fifth Avenue, and then go into the ranks just to show that there is no social side about them. Remember you are in a democratic country. Some of their ideas of duty are exactly opposed to ours. We take commissions to show our sense of responsibility: they refuse them to show their sense of sportsmanship. We're both right."

"I see the idea," said Blackadder approvingly, "so long as they don't all do it, of course—or what will their officers be like?" He continued to scrutinise the company. "What a lot of different uniforms. All the fifty-seven varieties of Allies—eh? See that bloke over there, with silver dummy cartridges all over his chest. A Serbian lieutenant, isn't he?"

"Yes, or a Roumanian. I'm not sure. One can't distinguish them all, these days. Here's our change. Come along."

The pair rose from their seats and made their way through the closely-packed tables towards the doorway. They were large men, and they attracted some attention. Winter heard his name called, and turned.

He found himself facing Geraldine Tilford, dining at a small table with Dale Conway. She looked prettier than ever, and radiantly happy.

" I believe you were going to cut me, Colonel Winter," she cried gaily. " Who is that officer with you ? He looks too lovely."

" He's an old friend of mine," replied Winter, with a glance at the hurriedly retreating back of the officer designated. " He's not usually shy, but I do believe you've frightened him away, Mrs. Tilford. We are a self-conscious race, you know, and he heard what you said."

" If it will soothe him any, you can say I was only referring to his uniform. Don't they look fine, all around the restaurant ? I was scolding Captain Conway here for not wearing his." She gave her dinner-companion a reproving frown, immediately discounted by a ravishing smile.

" All in good time, dear lady," said Conway. " When I was sent out here," he explained to Winter, " I was particularly warned not to bring a uniform with me, or I would risk intern-ment—if not interment ! "

" Quite right," said Winter. " But that's all over now. Uniform is going to be compulsory.

Well, I must go and look after my retiring friend. He has just arrived, and is feeling thirsty." He offered his hand awkwardly, hating himself for not being able to say something graceful.

"Are you coming to Captain Conway's lecture?" asked Geraldine, with an eager pressure from her slim fingers. "Carnegie Hall, next Thursday, for Allied War Charities. I have a box right next the stage. Will you be very sweet, and join my party?"

"Take a friend's advice, and stay away, Colonel!" said Conway, laughing. "It's the same old discourse as at Palm Beach, only longer."

"I will try to be there—but I'm working twenty-three hours a day just now," replied Winter. He had no particular desire to walk behind Conway's chariot again. "*Au revoir*, Mrs. Tilford, and thank you!"

"There," observed Conway, surveying Tom Winter's retreating form, "goes a man who would give his soul to be standing in my shoes! Who wouldn't, for that matter?"

He squeezed Geraldine's fingers exultantly.

"Now, don't be silly," she replied, highly flattered.

*　　*　　*　　*　　*

"Sorry to keep you waiting, old man," said Winter to his guest as he joined him in the lounge a moment later, "but you shouldn't be so coy. There was a pretty lady asking to be introduced to you."

For once Jimmy Blackadder was not interested in pretty ladies.

"Do you know that fellow dining with her?" he asked abruptly.

"Yes: he's a British War Lecturer. Some orator, I can tell you."

"Do you know his name?"

"I do. I met him at Palm Beach. His name is Conway—Dale Conway."

Jimmy Blackadder shook his grizzled head.

"Nothing of the kind," he said. "I recognised him the moment I set eyes upon him—even without his uniform. His name is Denis Cradock."

CHAPTER X   THE ELEVENTH COMMANDMENT

MR. MOON tapped at the door of the Artistes'
Parlour behind the spacious platform of Carnegie
Hall, New York City, and entered deferentially.
Mr. Moon had had cause to be deferential to
a good many people in the course of his life,
because, to employ a useful American idiom,
a good many people had got something on Mr.
Moon. To Dale Conway he paid the highest
deference of all.

"Good evening, guv'nor," he said.

"Come in, Moon," replied Conway. "Got the
medals?"

"These are the best I could manage. I
bought 'em from a Jew curio-dealer in Sixth
Avenue." Mr. Moon laid upon the table
certain British war decorations. Conway, in
immaculate civilian evening dress, examined
them.

"H'm! South African King's Medal. I am
more or less entitled to that, though I never
collected it. Crimean Medal. No, I think not:
it looks all right from a distance, but I shall
be at close quarters with various wise guys

to-night. The M.V.O.—Fourth Class, I should
say. That's always safe. Here's a Military
Cross : I wonder what poor devil had to part
with that—so soon! I think I *must* wear it.
What's this green and lake and white affair, I
wonder ? It looks like some Indian Frontier
contraption. Anyhow, I'll chance it. And here's
the Croix de Guerre. Yes, I think the French
Government might presumably have bestowed
that upon me. Here goes ! My word, I wish I
had had these in the Middle West ! " He arranged
the medals in their right order of precedence, and
pinned them neatly to the silk lapel of his coat.
" How's the house ? "

" Filling up fast, sir."

" And the money ? "

" I've told the cash-takers that I'll come round
during the lecture, and check their returns."

" And collect ? "

" Yes, sir—if they'll let me."

" They must let you. By the way, where's
the cash paid in advance for booked seats ? "

" I got that this morning, sir. It's at the
hotel."

" How much ? "

" About two thousand dollars."

" Not so bad. Add to-night's takings to
it, and I'll check it all up to-morrow morning :
I have to go out to supper after to-night's show.

Meanwhile, Moon, no fancy business with the petty cash, or anything of that kind, or it'll be the worse for you!"

"No, Captain Conway, sir," said Mr. Moon humbly. He was a small man, with a peaky face and a disillusioned expression. All his life he had allowed I Dare Not to wait upon I Would, with the result that at the age of fifty-six he was still serving as a private in the Crooks' Army.

"Now," continued Conway briskly, "go and wait at the back entrance—it's on Fifty-Sixth Street—and when my chairman arrives, bring him straight here."

"Yes, sir. Who is he?"

Conway mentioned a distinguished American name—a very distinguished name indeed. "He should be here about twenty minutes past eight : it's eight o'clock now. Slip round to Mrs. Tilford's box first, though, and see if the flowers are there for her. That's all."

There was a knock on the door—the door nearest the janitor's office. There was a second door, opening on to a passage which led to the platform and the Hall.

"Hallo!" said Conway. "Surely that isn't the chairman already."

It was not. It was Tom Winter, curiously quiet.

"May I come in?" he asked.

E*

Conway greeted him with effusion.

" This is jolly good of you, Colonel," he cried, shaking an entirely unresponsive hand. " I was feeling the want of a little moral support badly : Carnegie Hall is the biggest job I've tackled yet. Sit down and have a drink. This is Mr. Moon, my manager."

Colonel Winter surveyed the flinching Moon dispassionately.

" British subject ? " he inquired.

" Yes, sir."

" Old soldier ? "

" Oh, yes, sir." This was not true, but with Mr. Moon, the soft answer was the right answer.

Winter nodded. " I see." He turned to Conway. " Can you spare me five minutes ? "

" Certainly. Moon, go and wait for the chairman. Whisky and soda, Colonel ? "

" No, thank you." Winter sat down by the table. At his elbow lay the discarded Crimea Medal.

" I'll wet my whistle, if you don't mind : I have a heavy job ahead of me." Conway mixed himself a drink and lit a cigarette, humming cheerfully. His hand shook a little, for his intuitions seldom failed him.

Presently Winter spoke abruptly.

" You call yourself Dale Conway ? "

" Certainly."

" Since when ? "

" Since I came out here. A sort of *nom de guerre*, for lecturing purposes, and so on."

" Your real name, however," continued Winter, " is something entirely different."

Conway gave him a sudden glance ; then he smiled. He had a particularly confiding smile.

" Naturally," he said. " Perhaps you know it."

" Yes. It is Denis Cradock."

" Ah ! " said Conway thoughtfully, " Is it, now—is it ? "

" Yes. Under that name, at any rate, you served in the Army Pay Corps with the rank of Lieutenant, in Nineteen Fifteen."

" Did I ? "

" Yes. And in that capacity you absconded from France and made your way over to this country, with a considerable sum of money in your possession—not your own property."

Conway set down his glass with rather exaggerated deliberation, leant back in his chair, and knocked the ash off his cigarette.

" This is really all very interesting," he said. " Go on."

" Since then," pursued Winter, as steadily as ever, " you have made your way by representing yourself to be an emissary of the British Government, and so imposing upon American

hospitality. In other words, Mr. Cradock, you
are a common impostor."

Conway smiled indulgently.

" It's all a question of point of view," he said.
" I like you, Colonel, and I will be quite frank
with you. Let me ask you a plain question.
Aren't some of the people over here fair game ? "

" Not for a British officer and gentleman."

" That's a damned good answer, Colonel ;
but it doesn't go. I'm not an officer—I suppose
I was cashiered months ago—and I have long
perceived from your manner towards me that you
don't consider me a gentleman. So that's that !
Anyhow, can you blame me for trying to make a
bit while I get the chance ? "

Tom Winter was genuinely interested—and
attracted. Despite himself, he felt the fascination of the rogue's personality, particularly
his uncanny power to create an atmosphere
sympathetic to his own point of view. Presently
he spoke again.

" I am not disposed to question your right
to go to the devil in your own way—in peace
time. But don't you think the fact that we are
at war makes just a bit of difference, Mr. Cradock ?
Patriotism, and so on ! "

" Oh, certainly. But aren't you overlooking
the fact that I have done my bit already, with
something to spare ? Quite apart from the real

fillip that my lectures are giving to the Anglo-
American *entente* over here—you'll grant that,
won't you ? "

" I will—so long as you aren't found out."

" Trust me for that ! Quite apart, then, from
what we will call my propaganda value, I really
have done some soldiering."

" So I observe," replied Winter dryly, staring
at the medals upon Conway's evening coat.
" I notice that you were a member of the Tibet
expedition. It was a small expedition—one
might almost have called it select. I don't
seem to remember meeting you in Lhasa."

Conway glanced down at the green, lake and
white ribbon ; then across to his companion,
upon whose breast the same colours, among
numerous others, were disconcertingly visible.
Not that he was disconcerted.

" So that's what this medal is ! " he said,
smiling. " I was wondering. A funny coinci-
dence—eh, Colonel ? You and I are probably
the only two men in America who possess the
Tibet medal, and here we are sitting in the same
room ! "

Winter smiled too, despite himself. " But in
one direction," he said, " you have the advantage
of me. I was not in the Crimean War."

" Neither was I, to be frank : in fact, I wasn't
born. That little article on the table beside

you was a little bit of over-zealousness on my manager's part. He means well, but he is not up in dates." He glanced at his wrist-watch. " Now, Colonel, it's a quarter past eight, and I am expecting my chairman at any moment. Is there anything else you would like to say ? "

" Only one thing. You are under arrest."

Conway smiled, and shook his head.

" No, no—really ! " he said. " That is crude. Believe me, I have not pursued my present calling for all these years without acquiring a fair knowledge of the laws of the land in which I happen to be operating. You and I stand on an exactly equal footing upon American soil. You have no more power to arrest me than I have to arrest you."

" I had not last week," replied Winter, " nor even three days ago. But things have been moving since then. A definite military status over here has been granted to us by the Federal authorities, and I have just been appointed British Assistant Provost-Marshal for the New York district."

Conway whistled softly through his teeth. " The devil you have ! " he said. " Well, what are you going to do about it ? "

" Lock you up for the time being ; then ship you home for court-martial."

"Oh, no, you're not! Don't you believe a word of it!"

Winter rose to his feet. The gloves were off now, and his voice showed it.

"I am afraid we are wasting time, Mr. Cradock," he said. "I have the power to call in the police if I require them. Will you come with me quietly, like a sensible man, or must I—— ?"

Conway was on his feet too by this time.

"Colonel Winter," he said quickly, "you can't do this. I meant what I said just now. Don't you see you can't do it ?" His voice rose to a higher note.

"Why not ?"

"Do you realise," continued Conway, pointing, "that in the Hall through there three or four thousand people are waiting to hear me lecture ? If you arrest me now, what are you going to say to them ? Are you going to cry stinking fish ? Are you going to tell them that there will be no show to-night, because they've been played for a crowd of suckers by a crook—a British crook—a British officer crook ? Do you want the benches torn up ?"

"I shall tell your chairman that you have been taken suddenly ill—seriously ill."

"Yes, and the next thing you know there'll be twenty reporters round asking what hospital

I'm at. Do you think you'd be able to keep
a front-page story of that size from the ablest
pack of news-hounds in the world? Think
of the effect of such a scandal on our friends
here in New York—people who have dined
and wined us both. Do you want to make
them all feel damned fools—the laughing stock
of the other crowd, the crowd who tried to
dine and wine us and got frozen out? Haven't
you any consideration for them? And haven't
you any thought for the general consequences?
Don't you see that by hunting down an unfortunate devil like me at a moment like this,
when everything in the Anglo-American garden
is lovely, you are going to set back the *entente
cordiale* six months? Think, man—think!" He
gazed feverishly into Winter's face.

But Winter remained unshaken.

"Nevertheless, Mr. Cradock," he said, "you
are coming with me."

For a moment the two men eyed one another
intently—and who knows what thoughts were
in their hearts? Then Conway said suddenly:

"Look here—I've a plan to propose. There
is reason in my warning, and you know it.
From your own point of view, as I've said,
you will only be fouling your own nest if you
make a public example of me; and from my
own—well, of course, I don't particularly

want to be branded as an impostor and an ungrateful dog. I'll tell you what. Let me go on that platform now and give my lecture. The moment it is over, you can take me quietly into custody in this very room, and do what you like with me—and I'll take any sort of punishment that may be coming to me, without squealing. You can pass the word round, if you like, that I have been transferred to an appointment at home. There! That'll save everybody's face all round without robbing Justice of her rightful prey. What about it?" He gazed feverishly across the table. His breath was coming short and sharp.

Winter shook his head.

"The bargain is too much in your favour, Mr. Cradock," he said.

His retort had an unexpected effect. Without a word, Conway dropped into a chair and fell forward on to the table, with his face on his arms. Deep, shuddering sobs broke from him.

"*My* favour?" he sobbed. "My God! *My* favour?" He lifted a white, glistening face. "Do you know what I'm offering to give up? I have been a wanderer over the face of the earth for most of my life, penniless and friendless; and to-morrow my engagement was to have been announced to a lovely and wealthy woman who has actually told me that she cares for me—me!—a nameless adventurer struggling for a second chance! Yes, and we were to have been married in a fortnight! Is that nothing? To give up my happiness and a real home—is that a bargain in my favour? Oh!" he groaned again.

Tom Winter's tone softened—perhaps unconsciously.

"You mean—Mrs. Tilford?" he asked.

"Yes," replied Conway, looking up again. "You are going to humiliate her too! And I thought you were a friend of hers!"

It sounded like a mere empty reproach, but Conway watched eagerly for its effect. He was not disappointed.

Winter flushed a brick red.

"It is you who have humiliated her," he said. "What can we do that will save her now?"

Conway's brain, working furiously behind appealing eyes, noted the "we." He rose to his feet.

"Colonel," he said, "*mea culpa!* You're right; I have humiliated her. I had hoped, when we were married, to run straight and make good; but now that I have been shown up, that cannot be. I must forget her. I'm not kicking, it's not the first punch in the jaw that Fortune has dealt me. But Geraldine

—we *must* protect her, between us! I know you're a sportsman. She's in the Hall now, in a box, within a few feet of the stage. She organised the whole affair. We *can't* break her heart, as we would! Let me deliver my lecture! Let me have two words with her here after; and then—I'll put myself entirely in your hands."

Tom Winter surveyed him steadily.

" On your word of honour ? " he said.

" On my word of honour ! "

" Very well."

" Thank you, thank you, a thousand times ! " cried Conway. " It will mean the end of most things for me, but I appreciate the fact that you are behaving like a *sahib ;* and—we shall save little Gerry. I'll repay you, if I can."

There was a knock upon the outer door.

" That's Moon, with my chairman," said Conway. " I shall be on the platform in less than five minutes now." He opened the other door. " Here's a short cut. Bring her round directly after the lecture, will you ? *Au revoir,* and God bless you ! "

*   *   *   *

Winter left the room as Moon and the chairman entered. In a moment Conway was himself again—suave, cheery, and hospitable.

" Come right in, General," he said. " I can't tell you how I appreciate this honour. Sit down and mix yourself a drink, while I write a rather important note and arrange a few final details. We have about five minutes yet."

With his usual grace he made his guest entirely at home. Then he sat down, and after a brief moment of reflection scribbled a note.

" Come outside for a moment, Moon, he said. " There is a slight alteration in the programme."

I

AN hour and a half later, with the cheers of a vast audience in her ears and tears of proud gratification in her large blue eyes, Geraldine Tilford excused herself to her smilingly acquiescent guests and accompanied Tom Winter, by the private way, back-stage to the Artistes' Parlour. Here they found the sub-manager of the Hall.

" Where is Captain Conway ? " asked Geraldine eagerly.

" I guess he's saying good-bye to the chairman. I saw them going downstairs together. There's a considerable bunch outside asking for the Captain's autograph. I'm here to ascertain his general feeling on the matter. I'll go after him now—else the General will keep him talking all night."

" Tell him that Mrs. Tilford is waiting for him, will you ? " said Winter.

" Sure ! That ought to bring him ! " replied the manager gallantly.

The door closed behind him and the pair sat down.

"Isn't he perfectly wonderful?" said Geraldine, referring presumably to the recent lecturer.

"He's a marvel!" replied Winter, with perfect sincerity.

"That gift of his," continued Geraldine, with shining eyes—"how rare!"

"Perhaps it's just as well," replied Winter. He was answering mechanically. The thought of the blow which was shortly to be dealt to this radiant creature at his instance was trying his fortitude to the uttermost. His was a generous spirit; he felt thoroughly mean and despicable. How would she take it? he wondered. What would she do? Would she utter reproaches? Would she forswear men for ever? Would she follow Conway into exile? Or would she allow the incident to crush her completely, like the fragile blossom that she was? He did not know. He had little experience in the workings of a woman's soul. But one thing was tolerably certain—that friendship between Geraldine Tilford and the British Assistant Provost-Marshal of New York City was hereafter impossible.

Suddenly she became aware that she was speaking again, this time in a soft, shy, appealing voice.

"You've always been so sweet and chivalrous

to me, Colonel, and I want to tell you the news before anyone else. . . . You see, you are one of those quiet, protective men that all women must come to sometimes—when they are very happy, or very sad. A woman simply has to take her big joys and her big sorrows around to a man—sort of big-brother man—in the end. Well, Dale and I—— "

Tom Winter, suddenly conscious that he was about to be made the recipient of a confidence— a confidence as galling as it was unnecessary— rose to his feet.

" I say, Mrs. Tilford," he began awkwardly. " I don't think—— "

A footstep sounded outside the door.

" Talk of angels ! " he said, with a forced smile. " Here is Conway ! " He braced himself. It would be all over in a minute now. On the whole he was glad he had not tried to justify himself to her. Duty required—should require— no justification.

But it was not Conway. The sub-manager stood in the doorway. In his hand was a note.

" There has been some mix-up, Mrs. Tilford," he said. " Captain Conway drove away ten minutes ago. Gone back to his hotel, I guess. He left this for you." He laid the note upon the table. " Now I'll go back and break up

that crowd of autograph hounds. Good night ! ''
The door closed again.

Geraldine took up the note.

" That's strange," she said, with a puzzled
glance at Winter. She started. " Why, Colonel,
you look all white and scared. What has
happened ? "

" I expect that document will tell you," said
Tom Winter through his teeth.

Geraldine unfolded the note.

*Gerry, my dear—it said—I have broken the
Eleventh Commandment, which means the open
road again for me—as it would for most people.
Moreover, it means the end of you, so far as I
am concerned. Forgive me if you can, and
never trust a hard-luck story-teller again. I
advise you to marry Tom Winter, to whose
mistaken chivalry I owe my present get-away.
He is a solid citizen, and will never let you
down. Good-bye, my dear, dear Gerry, and
think of me as kindly as you can.*

D. C.

2

Meanwhile, in the cold and glimmering darkness of one of the subterranean platforms of the
Pennsylvania Station, beside the night sleeper
to Pittsburg, Mr. Moon was furtively handing

over certain moneys and documents to his employer.

"There's your transportation, guv'nor," he said, "and your upper-berth ticket. And here's the money—twenty-one hundred bucks that I had already, and about seven hundred, in this other bag, that I managed to collect from the Hall to-night. Some of the takers weren't too willing to part ; so I didn't press them."

"That's all right, Moon. We've done very well to hop it at all. By the way, what are you going to do with yourself now ? "

"I don't know, sir," said Moon, miserably.

"Well, clear out of New York. Chicago's the best place for you—or farther west. Got any money ? "

"About seventy-five cents, sir."

"You poor old fish ! It's a rotten world for small-time rogues. Here, take these ! " He began to count out ten-dollar bills from the lesser bag. "You'll have to keep pretty quiet wherever you go, or you'll get conscripted for a certainty ; and with your rabbit's heart you'll have a bad time."

Mr. Moon shivered.

"All abo—o—oard ! " The melodious chant of the negro Pullman porters came echoing down the platform, and the brakes came off the wheels with a reluctant sigh. Suddenly

Conway thrust the money back into the bag.

"Here, take the whole outfit!" he said. "You're a decent little chap, and I got you into this. Good-bye, Moon!" he thrust seven hundred dollars into Moon's limp hands, and swung on to the moving train.

"God bless you, guv'nor!" said the little man, with a sob.

*   *   *   *   *

Five minutes later, Denis Cradock, *alias* Dale Conway and heaven knows what else, late Army Pay Corps—rolling stone, soldier of fortune and human chameleon—rolled into his upper berth—a much-maligned resting-place, by the way—and composed himself to slumber.

"Good-bye, little Gerry!" he said. "You'll be happy enough with old Tom Winter—and you'd have bored me stiff in a fortnight! Still——"

He sighed, and fell sound asleep.

DENNY CRADOCK and Leo Bagby crossed the lawn from the river, towelling their heads vigorously. It was half-past eight on a June morning; and despite the fact that under the provisions of that gratuitous piece of officiousness, the Summer Time Act, it was really only half-past seven, the temperature was almost that of high noon.

Our friends, considerably increased in stature since we last saw them, were attired in pyjamas. Denny sported an ordinary red and white stripe; but Master Leo, whose tastes were more exotic, flew colours which put the roseate hues of early dawn to shame. They entered the open window, threw down their damp towels, after the manner of the eternal small boy, upon one of Mildred's spotless chair-covers, and cast appreciative eyes upon the harbinger of breakfast—a steaming jorum of porridge upon the sideboard.

As they appeared in the window, a neat ankle disappeared through the swing door leading to the kitchen. Denny noted the phenomenon, and stood for a moment rooted in contemplation. Leo, who was not interested in such matters at that hour of the morning, remarked :

" Hallo ! Post not come yet ? "

" No," replied Denny, gathering his wits ; " we're a bit rural up this backwater. We don't live in marble halls like Middlefield. Are you expecting a letter ? "

" Er—yes ; from my accountant."

" Chartered, or turf ? "

" The latter. Can I have some porridge ? "

" What—before you dress ? "

" Yes ; it's part of my system of diet." Ripening years had produced in Leo a curious fussiness about himself and his health, strongly reminiscent of that excellent but tiresome person his late mother. " Shall I explain it to you ? "

" No ! "

" Very well, then. If one takes porridge actually at breakfast, it cramps one's style for the remainder of the meal ; whereas if one takes it now, and then goes up to dress, it gives the porridge time to shake down, and so clears the track for more delectable fare."

" It must be an awful thing," said Denny, smoothing his hair at the mirror over the mantel-piece, " to go through life soliloquising about food. And why on earth don't you sit down when you eat ? "

Leo, impervious to these criticisms, continued to stand at the sideboard, gulping down porridge and cream with a tablespoon.

"There is a little Scottish blood in me," he explained. "Scotsmen always eat porridge standing up, and without sugar. I take sugar; otherwise I am whole-heartedly Caledonian in the matter of cereal food."

"You're a drivelling idiot," replied his friend dispassionately.

"Talking of food," continued Leo, "why were the festivities in connection with the twenty-first anniversary of your deplorable birth held last night? Are we going to have a second blow-out to-night, or what? By the way, I haven't wished you many happy returns yet. I now do so. Cheerio!" He waved his spoon in his host's direction.

"Thanks," said Denny. "We had to antici-pate a bit, on account of Molly: her half-term leave just fitted in. She goes back to clink this morning. I see Kent are putting it across Yorkshire."

"Hallo, have you got a paper?" Leo aban-doned his porridge bowl and leaned over the back of Denny's chair. "Does it say anything about the runners for the Gold Cup?"

"You are breathing porridge into my left ear," Denny pointed out. "As for the Gold

Cup, take the advice of an older and wiser man than yourself—— "

" I'm older than you, you ass."

" In years, possibly ; but remember that you are mentally extinct, and always have been— and keep away from horses. Stick to botany, or fretwork, or keeping white mice, or talking to yourself about your stomach ; but give up this habit of backing a loser every afternoon at three o'clock. Have your hobbies, my lad, but keep them at popular prices."

Denny rose and punched his friend playfully in the diaphragm. He was a lusty youth, a full head taller than Leo, and he no longer cherished any of his ancient respect for the latter's not inconsiderable sinews.

" Come and dress," he continued " We're going for a picnic lunch up Ripleigh Reach, for Uncle Tony's benefit."

" Ah, the old boy from India ? A trip on the river will do his liver a bit of no good. I enjoyed meeting him again last night : we had quite a long conversation. Really a very intelligent old fellow ! "

With these gracious and amiable words, Mr. Bagby disappeared in the direction of his bedroom. It was to be noted, however, that his host did not immediately follow him. Denny's eyes were again turned upon the swing door leading to the back premises. He stood before it in an attitude of abstracted meditation, with his feet rather far apart, caressing his upper lip with the tips of his fingers—a habit for which his mother and sister had frequently chaffed him, for as yet there was nothing to be seen there. However, as the door showed no disposition to resume its oscillations, Denny delivered himself of a sentimental sigh and went upstairs, whistling.

As so often happens in this life, the event for which he could not wait occurred directly after his departure. The swing door opened and the owner of the neat ankle reappeared. Her name was Simmons, and she was a pretty fluffily-fair damsel of about twenty, with large sentimental blue eyes and a silly but attractive mouth. There was nothing of the pert chamber-maid about her. She was a perfectly unsophisticated village girl, whom Mildred Cradock was trying to train into a good parlour-maid.

Simmons carried a tray, upon which reposed a massive tobacco jar and the morning's letters, most of which were naturally for Denny. Having deposited the jar in Denny's place, and buttressed it with correspondence, Simmons looked furtively around her and produced a small packet from the pocket of her apron. This she slipped under Denny's table napkin. Then, after a further glance in the direction of the staircase just outside the door, she tiptoed to the little table in the corner, where Mrs. Cradock kept the photographs of her three children, and having selected that of the son of the house, bestowed upon it a trembling kiss.

Next moment there came a light step upon the staircase. The guilty Simmons set down Denny and his silver frame as if they had been red hot, and made a dive for the empty porridge bowl of Leo Bagby, which reposed upon a chair near by. Joan Cradock entered—cool, summery, nineteen—radiant youth personified. She was smoking the pre-breakfast cigarette affected by this sophisticated generation.

" Has the post come yet, Simmons ? " she inquired.

" Yes, Miss," replied that quaking damsel. " It's nearly all for Mr. Denis this morning. This "—she indicated the tobacco jar—" is from all of us downstairs."

" I call that very nice of you," said Joan. " Mr. Denis will come and thank you after breakfast, I'm sure."

" Yes, Miss. I'll tell Cook," murmured the fluttered Simmons.

Joan laid a beribboned packet by Denny's plate, and sat down.

" Hallo," she remarked ; " someone has been breakfasting here already."

" Yes, Miss ; it was Miss Molly. She had her breakfast at eight, so as to catch the early train. She's upstairs now, getting her things on. I'll clear her place."

" Do," said Joan. " I loathe *débris*."

Simmons obediently removed all traces of Molly's early meal, and disappeared through the swing door. Joan helped herself to tea and toast, and proceeded to sip, munch, and smoke. There came another step on the stair, a mature and weighty step this time. Joan sprang to her feet.

" Good morning, Uncle Tony ! " she cried, and ran to the door.

Sir Anthony Fenwick had aged surprisingly little in seven years. He was an Englishman of a definite caste, with the philosophy of life peculiar to his order. He grumbled habitually, but never worried. Perhaps that was why the responsibility of steering an Indian province through all the swirling uncertainties of the War years had left so little mark upon him Anyhow, here he was home again, unfeignedly refreshed by the company of his niece and her stimulating family.

He accepted Joan's friendly peck, and patted her upon the shoulder.

" Good morning, Joan. Are we the first ? "

" Oh, no. There's been a perfect stream of

F

people pouring through this room all morning.
Denny, and Bags—— "

" Bags ? "

" Yes—Lionel Bagby. You met him at dinner
last night."

Uncle Tony helped himself to breakfast.

" Ah, that young gentleman. He told me
several things that I had not previously known
about the proper way to govern our Eastern
Empire. Your fiancé, I gathered ? "

Joan blew a reflective cloud of smoke.

" Well," she said calmly, " the matter has
hardly got beyond the committee stage, as yet."

" You mean—the local gossips are sitting
on it ? "

Joan nodded her shingled and shapely young
head.

" Yes. They are a large committee, and they
sit heavily. Laura Meakin is chairman. I don't
think they will decide anything for a long time
yet ; neither shall I."

" Wise girl, Joan ! But I seem vaguely to
recollect Master Bagby in a previous existence.
Have I met him before ? "

" Lionel the Terrible," said Joan. " But not
so terrible now, really "

" I remember. Rather fussy parents, unless
I am mistaken."

" Yes. But Mrs. Bagby died during the war

—rationing finished her off—and Mr. Bagby has married again. Something with serious views about life, and psycho-analysis. Complexes and inhibitions, and so on. Leo practically lives here now."

" I don't blame him. Wasn't there a sister ? "

" Yes—Gwen. Rather grand. She married the curate. Two babies."

" Wasn't that rather a blow for Denny ? "

" Oh, bless you, no ! Denny has had several affairs since then. He's a busy boy. One of these days he'll burn his fingers."

" You mean—— ?"

" Oh, nothing. I'm sorry mother isn't down : she's upstairs fussing over Molly. Molly really is a great blessing."

" She captured my elderly heart the first time I ever saw her," said Uncle Tony.

" Oh, I don't mean that way. Molly is a great convenience to Denny and me, because she loves being mauled about and mothered. A nice, affectionate, old-fashioned child, a safety-valve for Mother's maternal instincts. What are you gaping at ? "

" I apologise. You interest me so."

" Shock you, you mean ! "

Uncle Tony chuckled.

" Upon my word," he said, " I don't know ! "

" You soon will."

"The fact is, you are a new type to me. Having spent most of my life in the Orient—— "

"You regard me as an Occidental hussy? I'm sorry. This, for instance." Joan waved her cigarette. "Do you disapprove of women smoking?"

"Not in the slightest, so long as they do it in the right way."

"What do you mean?"

"In my young days it was a sign of good breeding in a man to keep his cigar or cigarette in his hand and not in his mouth. Nowadays I constantly see a man slouching into a public place, such as a restaurant, with six inches of cigar or cigarette-holder protruding from his face. Personally I would as soon think of coming in with my hat on. And of course what looks bad in a man looks worse in a woman."

Joan nodded thoughtfully.

"I see," she said. "I hadn't thought of it in that way."

"So I observed. With you, smoking is an elegant gesture. You don't sit with clenched teeth, emitting noxious vapours: you hold your cigarette prettily and naturally in your fingers, and it is a pleasure to watch you."

"You have got some nice ideas about things, Uncle Tony," said Joan—"especially about keeping your cigarette in your mouth being like a man wearing his hat in the house. Thank you for telling me that."

Uncle Tony smiled.

" My dear, I am proud to be able to tell this generation anything. Heigh-ho ! If Youth but knew ! " He wandered to the window and looked out. " Is that a car I hear ? "

" Yes, for Molly. I'll call her. No, here she is with Mother, at last."

Mildred bustled in, with Molly's arm in hers.

" You must think me a most neglectful hostess, Uncle Tony," she said, after the salutations inseparable from breakfast-time at Abbot's Mill, " but I was getting this child ready for her journey. Say good-bye, dear."

Molly, in the regulation blue serge and coloured hat-ribbon of schoolgirldom, approached her grand-uncle with solemn eyes. Her hands were behind her back. Joan, noticing, uttered a sisterly groan.

" Will you write your name in my autograph book, please, Uncle Tony ? " The words came with a rush.

" With pleasure."

> " The pestilential nuisances who write for
>   autographs ;
> All people who have flabby hands and
>   irritating laughs ;
> All children who——"

Joan caught her mother's eye.

"Sorry, Mum!" she said. "My sense of humour again!" And she composed herself meekly upon the sofa, with *The Daily Mirror*.

Meanwhile, Molly's mop-head had approached close to Sir Anthony's, and her gruff little voice was unfolding the mysteries of the autograph book.

"Don't write on those pages: they're only for girls, you know. Write on this one, or that. The pink is the nicest, I think. No, not on that: that's Lord Roberts' page."

"Where did you catch Lord Roberts?" asked Uncle Tony, contending with Molly's fountain pen, which was playing freely.

"I met him when I was *quite* little——"

"And what are you now?" Needless to say, the question came from the sofa.

"I'm nearly sixteen!" said Molly unexpectedly. In truth she looked more like twelve. "It was at a fancy fair, and I sold him a box of matches. When I told him that my father had fought under him in South Africa he gave me a kiss."

"The child was quite shameless," said Mildred proudly.

"And so Lord Roberts gets a page to himself," remarked Sir Anthony.

"No." Molly glanced towards Joan, and

lowered her voice. " There's another name there too," she said, in a husky whisper.

" I don't see it."

" It's—it's a pretend of mine. I like to believe it's there—that's all. I can't explain." Molly's face had grown very red.

" The child is mentally deficient, we fear," remarked a level voice from behind *The Daily Mirror*.

" Write your name next to someone you like," said Molly hurriedly.

" Do you think Rudyard Kipling would object if I put myself down in this corner, near him ? "

" I don't think he would a bit. He knows about India, too. Here's the blotting-paper. Thank you ever so much, dear Uncle Tony." A comprehensive embrace followed. " Mind you're here when I come home for the holidays."

" When will that be ? " inquired a strangled voice.

" The beginning of August."

" I will book the date forthwith."

" Come along, Littlest, or you'll lose the train ! " commanded Mildred, collecting sundry dropped belongings.

" All right, Mum." Molly dashed across to the sofa, kissed her elder sister, dashed back to kiss her uncle again, then dashed out of the room.

" Have you said good-bye to Denny ? " inquired her mother's anxious voice.

" Have you said good-bye to the cat ? " called Joan.

" Yes—upstairs," replied Molly, referring probably to her brother. " Have you got my sandwiches ? Thank you, Mum, dear. And chocolates ! Ooh ! "

Their voices died away. Joan rose, and lit a fresh cigarette.

" What a blessed thing is Youth ! " she said. " Uncle Tony, you are looking at me again."

" You are very easy to look at, my dear."

" I suppose the flippancy of this generation shocks you."

" Heaven forgive me, I rather like it ! I was just wondering where you got yours from. Not from your mother, I'll be bound."

" No. Mother is much too maternal to have any sense of humour. I don't think I can have got it from my father either."

" I never knew him."

" Neither did I, for that matter. At least, I was about two when he died. But from Mother's account of him he never sounded particularly frivolous." Joan sat suddenly up on the sofa, crossed-legged and serious. " Uncle Tony, what's your candid opinion of Ancestor

Worship ? Do you consider it a really sports-
manlike religion ? "

One of the likeable things about Sir Anthony
was his readiness to adapt himself to impulsive
changes of conversation.

" I have never come sufficiently in contact
with it, my dear," he said gravely, " to make
up my mind on the matter."

" Well, stay here a bit longer and you will ! "
Joan rose to her feet and began to walk about
the room, with her attractive boyish stride.
" This family of ours has been trained to model
itself day by day, year by year, upon a male
parent whom none of us can remember, and
whom one of us never even saw. We have
Father for breakfast, Father for lunch, Father for
dinner. He has been with us from our cradles :
he is a standing work of reference of the most
irritating kind. He never got his feet wet, or
employed slang expressions ; he never smoked
in bed, or left bills unpaid ; he was clean in
person, courteous to those of humble station,
and kind to animals. He went to church twice
on Sundays, and wore nice sensible under-
clothing all the year round. He must have
been a most exhausting person to live with.
Yet Mother worships his memory." She pulled
herself up suddenly. " Does that sound unfilial,
Uncle Tony, or irreverent ? "

F*

" It sounds very human, my dear."

" That's just the word ! I am awfully human,
and I can't worship a—a—what's the expression ? "

" An abstraction ? "

" That's right. I can't speak in a hushed
voice of the dead—especially the dead I never
knew. I suppose if I had known my father in
the flesh I shouldn't be talking like this : it
would be disloyal. Of course I never say these
things to Mother : it would hurt her. It's the
one thing she seems to be really sensitive about."

" I understand, my dear."

" We take some understanding," said Joan.
" We're a queer family."

" All families are queer. Even when they
are not, they like to think they are. But I
know how you feel. You and Master Denny
are modern, and you chafe under apron strings
—eh ? "

Joan nodded her head.

" Yes, that's it," she said. " And ancestors."

" They are much the same thing."

Joan nodded her head again.

" I suppose that's true," she said thoughtfully. " Do talk to Mother about them. Here
she is. Hallo, Mum ! Has your favourite child
departed at last ? "

" Isn't that a shame ? " asked Mildred of

Sir Anthony. " They know I have no favourites in this household ; and yet—— "

" 'Ere's a nice 'ot cup of tea for you, dearee,' said Joan soothingly.

" Thank you, darling. Of course Molly, being the old-fashioned one, responds a little more—— "

" All right, Mum ! It was only a leg-pull, as usual. Have you seen Denny's presents ? "

" No, dear." Mildred observed the tobacco jar for the first time. " What is this ? "

" That is from Cook, Jane, Tweeny, and Simmons, with a loving kiss."

" How good of them ! I must add mine to the collection. I'll just slip it under his napkin."

" My poor mother, you can't slip a cowhide suit-case under a folded napkin."

" He has had the suit-case," said Mildred, producing a sealed envelope a little guiltily. " This is just a small tip."

" I shall remember that when my turn comes ! " remarked her daughter darkly.

Mildred lifted the napkin.

" There's something here already," she said. " Another present—and it hasn't come by post. I wonder whom it is from. You, dear ? "

" No. My offering is the package with the red ribbon—a cigarette case. Perhaps it's from Molly."

"The child gave him hers last night. Was it you, Uncle Tony?"

"No. Mine is still in my pocket. It will be handed over shortly, accompanied by an improving discourse from Godfather."

"I wonder if it would be fair to have a peep at it," suggested Mildred.

"Why not?" said Joan, taking the packet.

"He'll be terribly cross if he catches us."

"Never mind, chance it!" Joan unrolled the paper and disclosed a horseshoe scarf-pin.

"What a funny little present!" said Mildred.

"Nine-carat gold!" commented Joan.

"With an inscription. What does 'Mizpah' mean, I wonder?"

"It means," remarked Joan, with a sidelong glance towards the swing door, "that Master Denny is getting rather a big boy." She turned suddenly upon her uncle. "What sort of discourse are you going to deliver to him, Uncle Tony?"

"I don't know. Can you suggest a text?"

"I could, but I won't."

"I shall be so glad if you *will* say a word to him, Uncle Tony," interposed Mildred. "I was wondering only this morning what advice his father—— "

Joan rolled up her blue eyes towards the ceiling.

" Now we've done it, Uncle Tony ! " she said.

" Done what, my dear ? "

" Started Mother. Ancestor Worship has commenced for the day ! "

Further irreverence was prevented by the entry of Denny himself, followed by Leo, both immaculate in white flannels. Mildred embraced her son.

" Denny, dearest," she said, " bless you ! Have a happy birthday ! "

For a moment Denny's schoolboy reserve melted, and he hugged his mother, nursery fashion. Then he acknowledged the congratulations of his uncle and sister, and turned to the table.

" Presents ! " he exclaimed. " Loud applause !"

The next few minutes were devoted to the tearing asunder of parcels ; after which, at the earnest solicitation of Mr. Bagby, Denny ceased throwing brown paper about the room and sat down to bacon and eggs. It is to be noted, however, that he made no reference to the horseshoe scarf-pin.

" Eat up your breakfast quickly, boys," said Mildred. " I want you to get the launch ready : we're going to take Uncle Tony up Ripleigh Reach."

" Picnic lunch ? " inquired Joan.

" Yes."

" That means," explained Joan to Sir Anthony,

" that about one o'clock you will find yourself sitting on a wasp's nest, eating chicken salad with a fountain pen. You two lads had better have some more sausages, to pull you through the day. You coming too, Mother ? "

" Oh, yes, I must be with you to-day. I'll run off and perform my household duties now, and get them over."

" Run rapidly," advised Joan, glancing out of the window, " or Laura will catch you ! "

" Laura Meakin ? " exclaimed Mildred. " Oh dear ! "

There were panic-stricken exclamations from all parts of the room.

" Who is Laura Meakin ? " inquired Sir Anthony.

" The Human Blister," replied Denny.

" She was away last time you were here. I think," said Mildred. " I seem to remember——"

" I bet she's going to make up for lost time now," remarked Joan. " Be absolutely firm with her, Uncle, and if necessary, brutal ! "

" Don't promise to take the chair at anything," said Denny.

" And mind you don't breathe a word about the picnic, or she'll come too," added Joan.

" Here she is," hissed Denny. " Take cover ! "

A firm step crunched the gravel outside, and Miss Laura Meakin appeared in the window.

MOST families have a Laura Meakin. Laura's outstanding characteristic was an uncompromising sense of duty : much of her crowded, energetic, and mainly futile existence had been devoted to correcting in Mildred's offspring the faults incident upon their mother's manner of bringing them up. With Joan and Denny she waged continuous warfare, and they treated her with the frank rudeness due to a declared and invulnerable opponent.

" Good morning, everybody ! " Laura was a lady of commanding presence, attired in country garments of an eminently sensible nature—thick boots, massive walking-stick, and a masculine felt hat.

Mildred, who pitied all childless people, and was constitutionally incapable of discourtesy to anyone, advanced to greet her with her usual ready smile. Mildred's children, with the candour of youth, made no attempt to assume any appearance of cordiality whatsoever.

" How nice of you to look in, dear," said Mildred. " This is my uncle, Sir Anthony

Fenwick. Uncle Tony, this is Miss Meakin, our nearest neighbour and an old friend."

" How do you do ? " said Uncle Tony, rising and shaking hands.

" I have a slight cold in the head," replied Laura, who was a person of literal disposition. " I suppose you arrived for the dinner last night ? " She turned to her hostess. " I was expecting you to invite me too, Mildred, but of course, old friends are easily dropped. Joan, I have spoken to you before about cigarette smoking."

" Yes, Laura," replied Joan, with a seraphic smile, " and I promise you many opportunities of doing so again." She produced a powder-puff and mirror, and embarked upon one of the public toilet exercises to which this generation is so frankly addicted.

" You know it will ruin your teeth in time," pursued Laura, unswerving in her duty. " Your complexion is going already : anybody can see that."

" There's plenty more where it came from thank you, dear," replied Joan, busy with the puff. Laura, squarely repulsed, swung round towards the table.

" Good morning, Denis ! " she said. " You have now reached years of discretion. It was time ! "

" Thank you so much for pointing it out," replied Denny politely. He indicated his friend

with the handle of his knife. " You know Bags,
I think ? "

" I cannot endure childish nicknames,"
Laura reminded him. " Good morning, Mr.
Bagby ! "

Leo Bagby, taken rather at a disadvantage by
reason of a thoughtless mouthful of sausage,
rose to his feet, made an affable noise, and sat
down again.

" In my young days," said Laura, " gentlemen
were not accustomed to speak to ladies with
their mouths full. But perhaps Joan "—she
turned to observe the effect of this side thrust,
fruitlessly—" has not been educated to expect
such courtesies." She turned to Denny again.
" I have a birthday present for you." She
extracted a square package from her ample
coat pocket.

" What sort ? " inquired Denny cautiously.
" Tracts ? "

" It is a recently published work upon Social
Service, by a personal friend of mine. She has
been kind enough to autograph it for you, on the
front page."

" Thank you very much," replied Denny,
accepting the volume dubiously. " Have I got
to read it ? "

" Certainly. It will do you good. It will do
you all good."

" Then we'll let Mother read it first," announced
Denny, with a smile of happy inspiration. " Have
a banana ? "

" I think you know," said Laura coldly " that
I do not eat uncooked fruit."

" Well, have a baked apple, or a chair, or
something ! " said Denny.   " Let us be convivial,
for Gawd's sake ! "

" I will sit down for a moment," replied
Laura, " because I have some business to discuss."
She planted herself heavily upon the sofa,
beside the flinching form of Uncle Tony.   " It's
about the Meeting."

" The Meeting, dear ? " asked Mildred, a little
apprehensively.

" Yes—the Meeting of the Society."

" Forgive me asking, but which ? " inquired
Denny.

" Your interests are so diversified," explained
Joan politely.

" The League of Educative Science."
There was an interval of respectful silence.
Then Joan inquired :

" What is that, if anything ? "

" Stinks," said Denny promptly.

" Denny, Denny ! " said Mildred

" Sorry, Mother ! "

" He means Chemistry, Miss Meakin," explained
Leo, hastening characteristically to the rescue

"But I do not mean Chemistry," said Laura. "I mean Social Science."

"Never heard of it," replied Denny.

"I will explain, Miss Meakin," announced Leo, one of whose hobbies was the involved elucidation of the obvious.

"Thank you, I am quite capable of explaining myself." Miss Meakin turned impressively upon Sir Anthony, who immediately adopted an attitude of massive concentration. "One of our activities is to instruct the mothers of the village in the scientific rearing of children."

"What do you instruct the grandmothers of the village in?" flashed Denny, before anyone else could speak. "Sucking eggs? Sorry, Mother!"

"What else does the Society do?" inquired Sir Anthony, in a solemn voice.

"It maintains Recreation Centres, where children are taught to amuse themselves rationally and scientifically."

"Poor little mites!" This from Joan.

"The Annual Meeting," pursued Laura, oblivious of these ribald interruptions, "is to be held this day fortnight. I want to have it in this house, Mildred."

"Oh dear!" exclaimed Mildred. "I mean——"

"The bomb," announced Denny to Leo Bagby, "has now exploded."

" I mean, certainly ! " continued Mildred,
recovering herself.   " What—what date will that
be ? "

" The fifteenth of July."

" The fifteenth ?   Let me think.   I have a
feeling that something is happening on that
date already."

Corroboration was immediately forthcoming
from the breakfast table.

" I should think something was happening !
The Regatta ! "

Mildred gave a little sigh of relief and turned
to Laura.

" There, dear ; you see—— "

" I selected the date on purpose," announced
Laura calmly.

" Are the Society going to teach the crews
how to row ? " inquired Joan.

" I have selected that date," pursued Laura,
" because everybody of importance in the
district will be here.   The Regatta ends about
six, and nothing happens after that except
a lot of unnecessary eating and drinking "—she
rolled a cold eye in the direction of the breakfast
table—" until the fireworks commence at nine.
The Meeting can be at a quarter past six."
She rose to her feet.   " Then that's settled."

" I suppose so, dear," said Mildred resignedly.

" Thank you. By the way, we haven't got a

chairman yet. Will you be here, Sir Anthony?"

"No!" shouted Joan and Denny together.

"I hope Uncle Tony will be here," remarked Mildred gently, "but we don't want to commit him to public appearances at present. He's having a holiday."

"Well, I shall see," said Laura calmly. "Now I must be off : I have some Old Age Pensioners to visit. You shouldn't wear blue, Mildred ; it doesn't suit you. I have spoken to you about it before. Good-bye!"

She strolled through the window, and the sound of her resolute footsteps died away. The Cradock family promptly indulged in extravagant manifestations of relief from strain.

"Old maids' children!" remarked Joan, swinging her legs over the arm of her chair.

"Social Stinks!" mumbled Denny.

"Now, don't be uncharitable, children," said Mildred, who never quite gave up hope of reforming her family. "Laura is a very good woman. I wish I had her courage."

"I wish I had her nerve!" said Joan.

"I wish I had her moustache!" said Denny, with obvious sincerity.

"What do you think of the League, Uncle Tony?" asked Joan.

Sir Anthony puffed thoughtfully at his pipe.

"There is quite a vogue for that sort of

interference with other people's comfort nowadays," he said. " How you can educate children to make mud pies, or play hopscotch, or drown kittens in a canal rationally and scientifically beats me. Still, it may keep them out of worse mischief."

" The children ? "

" No. The Society ! "

" You're as bad as the rest, Uncle Tony ! " sighed Mildred.

Sir Anthony laughed, and patted her upon the shoulder.

" Temporary demoralisation, produced by bad company—that's all ! " he said. " When does the aquatic adventure start ? "

" As soon as possible. Boys, go and get the launch ready : the lunch baskets are in the hall."

" Righto ! " said Denny. " Bags, old friend, you have eaten enough. Give us a hand, Joan."

The resisting guest was uprooted by his hosts and escorted, still masticating, out of sight and hearing.

Mildred sat down upon the sofa beside Sir Anthony. They smiled upon one another understandingly.

" You're a happy woman, Mildred."

" Who wouldn't be, with my children ? "

" They certainly are a credit to somebody. All done by kindness and Ancestor Worship ! "

Mildred shook a finger at him.

" You've been talking to Joan ! "

" Joan may have been talking to me," admitted Uncle Tony guardedly.

Mildred knitted her brows.

" Joan is a little inclined to be restive under my old-fashioned methods," she said ; " but Ancestor Worship has been more of a help to her than she realises. It's not easy for young people to keep to the right in line these days, Uncle Tony. It's a terribly dangerous age that they live in. Do you realise that ? "

" You mean—so much liberty—licence ? "

" Yes—especially for girls. Joan could get into all sorts of mischief if she wanted to ; and I think she sometimes does want to. She is more temperamental—horrid word !—than you would think. But I believe I have taught her what her father would have taught her— that it would not be playing the game to take advantage of the complete liberty I give her to do anything—common."

" I see."

" She's a terribly modern child, of course— utterly outspoken about other people, and utterly reticent about herself. Now Molly "— Mildred's brow was suddenly unravelled—" is a particularly satisfactory child to have. She positively enjoys confiding in her mother."

" It's a good thing you have no favourites ! " said Uncle Tony solemnly.

" And it's true ! Only,"—there was a curious tremor in Mildred's voice now—" Molly seems to belong to me more than the other two. You see, she came to me after—after I became a widow ; and that makes me feel solely responsible for her, somehow. No, Molly's no trouble ; Denny is my anxiety. He's a nice, amiable, amusing boy ; but he's terribly weak—especially where a pretty face is concerned."

" Did you ever know a man who wasn't ? "

" Were you ? "

" I was," replied Sir Anthony majestically—" and am ! " He kissed his niece. " Denny's all right : he'll settle down. Don't worry, my dear."

" I try not to," said Mildred, with a little sigh.

" On the contrary, you should rejoice. Now, I'm going into the garden to excogitate a suitable birthday homily for my godson. My chief difficulty will be to select a text."

" I'll come and help you to find him," said Mildred : " he's probably down at the landing-stage by this time. Then I must come back and collect a few umbrellas and waterproofs. No one in this house will do it if I don't—and you know what an English summer day can be ! I'll ring for Simmons to clear breakfast. Dear Denny ! It's ridiculous to think he's twenty-one ! "

Mildred took her uncle's arm, and the pair disappeared into the garden.

* * * * *

Simmons entered with the tray and began to clear away breakfast. Her first proceeding was to examine Denny's place at table, from which, she observed with a fluttering heart, her birthday present had disappeared. Almost at the same moment the recipient of the gift came softly down the staircase and entered the room. His rubber-soled boating-shoes made no sound. He halted in the doorway, reddened, and gazed fondly upon the pre-occupied Simmons. Then, under sudden impulse, he stepped forward and put his hands over the girl's eyes.

Simmons gave a terrified little yelp, broke away, and whirled round.

" Oh ! " she whispered. " It's you, Mr. Denis, dear ! "

" Yes, it's me," admitted Denny. " But I told you not to call me Mr. Denis." He stepped forward again and, conquering the fundamental diffidence of the youthful male, put his arms round her. Simmons submitted passively. Passive submission was her principal charm in Denny's eyes : what lovers of twenty-one chiefly dread is a rebuff.

" Did you give me that horseshoe present ? "
he asked.

" Yes, sir."

" Yes, dear ! "

Simmons wriggled shyly, then made the effort.

" Yes—dear ! Did you like it—dear ? "

" I thought it was absolutely topping. Er—
I say—you are a little darling, aren't you ? "

" Am I ? "

" Yes. I simply can't resist you."

" Oh ! "

Deeply gratified, Miss Simmons buried her
face timidly in Denny's shoulder.

" I simply can't resist anyone," continued
Denny, with more candour than tact, " who is
fair and fluffy."

" Just anyone ? " asked Simmons, looking
up sharply.

" I don't *love* any of them, of course," Denny
hastened to add. " I only love you."

" Really ? "

" Yes, really."

Simmon's face was upturned now, and very
close. The moment had arrived. Summoning
all his manhood, Denny kissed her. Simul-
taneously there came a stifled exclamation from
the open window, where Mildred and Uncle
Tony, deep in conversation, had just drifted
into view.

DENNY leaped back a clear four feet. Simmons uttered a muffled shriek, and bolted through the swing door like a panic stricken blonde rabbit.

" H'm ! " said Uncle Tony. " I have found my text ! "

" Oh, Denny ! Denny ! " cried Mildred, genuinely distressed.

Denny raised distracted fists heavenward.

" Mother ! Mother ! " he cried. " I wonder why God made all girls so pretty ! "

" A most apposite reflection," observed Sir Anthony. " You are not the first who has made it either, Denny."

By this time Mildred had recovered most of her usual cheerful composure.

" I'm sorry you did that, old man," she said. " Simmons is a feather-headed little thing, but a very decent girl. Now she will have to go ; and I may find it difficult to get her as good a place as this. Wasn't it a little bit—selfish ? "

" Yes," said Denny, all contrition now ; " I can see it was—rottenly ! But it's awfully hard to resist them, mother—especially when they're—— "

" I know. But is it the game ? Is it up to the standard ? You know the standard I mean ? "

Mildred walked slowly out of the room and upstairs, with an appealing backward glance in the direction of Uncle Tony. That embarrassed diplomat cleared his throat in a distressing fashion, and gazed awkwardly upon his godson.

" We will now improve the occasion," he said. " Will you smoke a cigar ? "

Denny declined, but he appreciated the gesture. Uncle Tony was not going to treat him as a child : it was to be man's talk.

" Don't you think, Uncle Tony," he said presently, " that mother's standards are a bit high ? "

" Women's standards are always higher than men's, Denny. That is why, when they fall from them, they come down more heavily than we do."

" But the standards mother sets up for me are supposed to be my father's standards, and —well, things have changed since his time. Very few of my friends seem to have any standards at all ; they have a lot of fun instead. It's a rotten job," concluded Denny ruefully, " being a righteous man in a wicked world."

Uncle Tony lit his cigar reflectively.

" Are you quite sure it is such a wicked world, Denny ? "

" Well—look at it ! "

" If this world were as wicked as it would have you believe it would have perished—collapsed upon itself—centuries ago. Humanity—the sort of humanity that you and I mix with—isn't really depraved. It's only timid."

" Timid ? "

" Yes—timid and sheep-like. Denny, there are far more good people walking this earth pretending to be bad than bad people pretending to be good. There's nothing makes a poor human sheep feel so safe as trying to make a noise like a wolf. That has been my experience over and over again. Scratch a devil of a fellow, and in nine cases out of ten you'll find a man with the soul of a churchwarden doing his darnedest to avoid being found out. So—never be discouraged by appearances. That's my philosophy of life. Incidentally, there's my birthday homily safely off my chest ! Now "—Uncle Tony suddenly produced an envelope from his pocket—" here you will find a small cheque, which my banker may or may not cash—— "

" Oh, I say, Uncle Tony ; thanks most awfully ! " cried Denny, all of a schoolboy again

" ——And good luck to you in life ! May the

gods give you two things :—rather more work than you can comfortably do, and an absolutely reliable sense of humour. They are about all a man really needs in this world. And—always play the game by your mother."

Unmanly tears sprang to impulsive Denny's eyes.

"I will, Uncle—I will! By Jove, you are a sportsman! And I'm sorry about that little girl : it was a mouldy thing to do. I'm afraid I'm rather a rotter at times," he continued, in an unaccustomed mood of self-abasement. "I sort of give way to things, suddenly. Luckily, with my family history-sheet, it can't be anything very deep."

"You regard your malady as functional, not organic, eh?"

"I don't know what that means ; but I'm sure you're right. Do you mind shaking hands, Uncle?"

CHAPTER XV   HOSTAGES

TEN minutes later Simmons, still a little pink
about the eyes and inclined to intermittent
chokings, ushered a visitor into the empty
morning-room.

He was an attractive-looking, clean-shaven,
well-set-up man of about forty-five, dressed
in a blue serge suit. The suit was smart and
well cut, but inclined to be shiny at the seams.

The stranger looked round the sunny room,
with its bright chintzes and flowers, with obvious
interest and appreciation. Then he turned to
Simmons, and stood surveying her in an attitude
of abstracted meditation, with his feet rather
far apart, caressing his upper lip with the tips
of his fingers.

" A pleasant morning," he remarked affably.

" Yes, sir. They are all going on the river ;
but I think Mrs. Cradock is still upstairs. What
name shall I say ? "

The stranger reflected.

" Mrs. Cradock won't know it, but you can
say Captain Conway—Captain Dale Conway."

" Yes, sir."

191

Simmons turned to go, but found Captain Conway standing between her and the door, gazing down upon her with manifest approval in his bold grey eyes. Simmons dropped her own nervously, and sniffed.

" Are you in distress, my dear ? " inquired Captain Conway.

" Oh, no, sir ! "

" I always like to help little girls in distress."

" Thank you, sir."

" Especially when they are fair and fluffy. I never can resist them when they are fair and fluffy."

To prove his words the visitor laid a paternal hand upon Simmons's shoulder. The result was an agitated squeal and another hurried exit. Masculine admiration was meat and drink to Simmons, but it is possible to have too much of a good thing in the course of a single morning.

Captain Conway now put his hands in his pockets and strolled round the cheerful room, humming a little tune. Presently he came to the sideboard, upon which stood a silver cigarette box. He helped himself to a cigarette and, having lit it, replenished his own case from the same source. Afrer that he continued to stroll, halting next at the small table beside the mantelpiece, upon which stood the portrait gallery of the Cradock family. He had inspected

Denny with obvious interest, and was upon the point of carrying Joan over to the window for better light, when he was aware of a footstep in the doorway behind him. He did not turn, but looked up into a Venetian mirror on the wall.

"Good morning, Mildred!" he said. "The bad penny has turned up!"

Mildred Cradock halted in the open doorway, with her hand on her heart, and terror in her eyes.

"Denis! You!" she whispered hoarsely.

"At your service," replied her husband, taking his stand before the mantelpiece, cigarette in mouth, hands in pockets.

She advanced towards him—a few dazed, uncertain steps.

"I thought you were dead!"

Denis Cradock smiled.

"Ah, did you? That was rather a liberty, Milly. You appear disappointed that I am not."

"I am." Mildred had characteristically resumed control of herself.

"Why? Have you married again? No, of course not: that's a stupid question: otherwise you wouldn't still be Mrs. Cradock. It was by that name I traced you here."

Mildred spoke again. Her deep voice was pitched a little higher than usual: otherwise it was expressionless.

G

" Where have you been ? Where have you come from ? "

" Recently, from Southern California. Generally speaking, from going to and fro in the earth and wandering up and down it. That is a quotation from Scripture, which you may or may not regard as apposite."

" What do you want ? "

" Want ? What do you think I want ? " Cradock spread his arms abroad comprehensively. " The comforts of home."

" Where is that—woman ? "

" Could you be a little more explicit ? There are so many—women."

" The woman you took away in that boat, with its bribed crew."

" Oh, that lady ? Well, as a matter of fact she took me away. She bribed the crew, too. I had no money : I never have ! But I can set your mind completely at rest so far as she is concerned. I haven't seen her for more than fifteen years. She proved to be a quite impossible person, I regret to say. Don't you worry about her. At present I am absolutely heart-whole. In the words of the poet, ' All that I ask is Love ; All that I want is You ! ' " He threw his cigarette into the fender and took a step nearer. " Milly ! "

Mildred stepped back a corresponding distance.

" Keep your distance, my man ! " she said calmly.

" Certainly," replied Cradock, sitting down. " It's rather a warm morning. Could I have a little refreshment, do you think ? Thank you ! " He leaned over and rang the bell.

Mildred remained standing.

" Keep your distance," she repeated, " and keep silent while I speak to you. I am not afraid of you. After what you did that night, on that ship—— "

" Dear, dear ! Feminine jealousy lives long, doesn't it ? "

" I am not speaking about that poor creature : she was welcome to you. I am speaking of something different."

The swing door opened behind her, and Simmons appeared.

" Did you ring, ma'am ? "

" Yes. Will you bring the whisky and soda for Captain Conway, please ? "

" Yes, ma'am."

Simmons disappeared, and Conway inquired :

" Something different, eh ? What was that ? "

" I was thinking," said Mildred, " of the way in which you, an officer and gentleman—— "

" I wasn't a real officer, you know," said Conway, with a ready smile ; " only a Squadron Commander in some Irregular Horse—some extremely Irregular Horse. Their irregularity, especially off duty, was quite unique." He chuckled, like a schoolboy—like Denny.

"You were responsible." pursued Mildred steadily, " for the safety of a company of British soldiers."

"A half-company ; but you are wrong in any case. As it happened, I was not travelling on duty, but on leave, and in mufti. The men in question had their own officer to look after them. In spite of that fact, I took the trouble, when the alarm was given, to see that they were paraded upon that portion of the deck provided for such an emergency."

"It was your duty, as senior officer on board," pursued Mildred relentlessly, " to stay until the last man was rescued."

Cradock nodded his head thoughtfully.

"A nice point," he said ; " but I think you are wrong. I had other duties."

"Duties ? " For the first time Mildred permitted herself an ironical smile.

"Yes. In a case of this kind the procedure is simple and invariable—women and children first. I observed that you and the two children were being well looked after—in fact, it hurt me a little to observe what a lot of men seemed to be doing it—so I took steps to ensure the safety of the only other woman on board whom

I happened to know. After that, I considered that I was entitled to look after myself. Still, I respected your susceptibilities to the last, Milly—and I think you might be a bit more grateful about it."

" What do you mean ? "

" I mean this. When we were picked up a few days later, I gave my name as Arthur Swann."

" Not Conway ? "

" No. Dale Conway was one of my later incarnations. Anyhow, Denis Cradock disappeared from the pages of history—or rather from the books of his creditors, who realised with profound relief that they had touched bottom at last—without permitting his name to be associated in any way with that of any lady but his wife. Don't thank me : I liked doing it. However, that's all ancient history now. No doubt you would like to hear of some of my more recent adventures. Would you ? "

" No ! " replied Mildred decisively.

But here Simmons entered with the prescribed whisky and soda, and the only alternative to constrained silence was small talk.

" What happened to you during the war, Captain Conway ? " asked Mildred, sitting down at last. " I suppose you rejoined at once."

" Indeed, yes. I had a most interesting time."

" What front were you on ? "

" I was on the Western Front to begin with. Thank you, dear ! "   This to Simmons, proffering a sizzling glass.

" In the Cavalry ? "

" Not this time : they thought I was too old. Absurd, of course, but one has to accept these things. They put me in the Army Pay Corps."

" How dangerous," said Mildred. " For the Army, I mean," she added, as the door swung to behind Simmons.

" Don't be catty, my dear. It may have been dangerous for the Army, but it was equally dangerous for me. I took all sorts of risks."

" I don't doubt it."

" In fact, my fondness for risks landed me in serious trouble."

" A surprise visit from the auditor ? "

Conway laughed, good-temperedly.

" Have the last word, by all means," he said. " As a matter of fact, what happened was this." And he proceeded to repeat for his wife's edification the stirring tale of the field cashier's car, Hellblast Corner, and the ten-franc notes.

" Did they find any of the money ? " asked Mildred when he had finished.

" None. Most of Belgium is under water during the winter."

" And what sentence did they impose ? "

" I did not stay to listen. As I sat waiting in the empty hut for the General to make up his mind on the subject, it suddenly occurred to me that—to employ a popular expression of the period—I had done my bit. So I got up, walked out to my unguarded car, stepped on board, and set off for New York."

" New York ? "

" Yes—via Havre, where I contrived to bluff my own way on board a French liner, which conveyed me across the Atlantic."

" First class, of course ? "

" Certainly."

" You could well afford the money ! "

" It is a rule of the British Army, Milly, that officers in uniform must travel first-class. Not that I wore uniform after I stepped upon neutral soil—that would have been both useless and dangerous. However, that by the way. I may say, in all modesty, that I was a great success in America. I was quite a little pet ; you would have been proud of me. The Americans are an extraordinarily hospitable people, and they appreciate an Englishmen who is what they call ' a good mixer.' If he happens to be a wounded hero into the bargain—— "

" You were wounded ? " asked Mildred quickly.

" Yes ; I forgot to tell you that.   I had been gassed.   When lecturing I used to stop and cough sometimes ; that was a great help.   Kind-hearted folk used to come round behind the platform after my lectures, with tears in their eyes, and press me to accept an extra hundred dollars.   I did so ; but I was almost ashamed to take the money.   But of course the market was soon spoiled.   The game was so attractive that blundering out-siders butted in and ruined it.   Then America came into the war herself, and that gave our military authorities an official footing in the country."   Denis Cradock wriggled, as if under some disagreeable reflection.   " Official—and officious.   Damned officious ! "

" What did you do when you were found out ? " asked his wife calmly.

" I trekked farther west—to California.   I worked in moving pictures there for some months. A most attractive spot."

" Oh, why, why did you leave California ? " Mildred was speaking from her heart this time.

" For that very reason.   Work—too much of it !   As you know, the sight of work always makes me feel sick and faint.   Besides, I was such a good rider and swimmer that I was constantly being detailed for laborious stunts like battles and shipwrecks.   It wasn't a job for a gentleman at all. And "—the speaker shrugged his shoulders—" there were other inconveniences."

"Someone's husband began to make trouble, I suppose?"

"On the contrary, he was much too accommodating. He offered to retire permanently in my favour!" Cradock leaned forward, shaking an impressive forefinger. "My dear Milly, the looseness of the marriage tie in some of those Western States is nothing more or less than a public scandal. Lay a finger on it, and it comes undone in your hand; and you find yourself roped in as Husband Number Two before you know where you are! No, I wasn't having any. So I boarded the next train and came home—to you!" He leaned back again, glass in hand, with a satisfied smile. "There— frankly, freely, and without extenuation—you have the history of your rolling stone, tossed by the hand of Fate into this sleepy little backwater of yours. *A toi!*" He emptied the glass and set it down again. "And now—what about it?" he asked briskly.

His wife rose from her seat, and stood looking thoughtfully down upon the handsome, lined, impudent face that smiled up at her.

"And you have been going through the world all these years," she said—and there was real

G*

pity in her eyes—" lying, cheating, cadging, pilfering ? "

She had fairly flicked him on the raw this time. The smile faded, and Cradock sprang to his feet.

" Come, come, Milly," he cried, " don't be a little hypocrite ! You know my creed. The world's my oyster—my big, fat, luscious, not particularly sensitive oyster. All mankind are fair game. If my neighbour is fool enough to let me pick his pocket, he has no one to blame but himself. If ever I meet a man clever enough to pick my pocket, I shall let him do so with pleasure. What could be fairer than that ? Life, my dear, is not a picnic, as you in this up-river existence of yours appear to imagine ; it's a campaign—a campaign for most of us against power and place and privilege. What have I ever had "—his voice trembled with genuine emotion ; characteristically he had moved himself, but not his wife—" to help me in the battle of life ? Wealth, birth, influence ? Nothing of the kind ! Nothing but my five wits, and a perfect digestion ! "

" May one add—a thick skin ? " suggested Mildred gently.

Denis Cradock caught up the retort with characteristic dexterity.

" A thick skin comes under the heading of a

perfect digestion," he said. " The first symptom
of indigestion, I'm told, is remorse. No, my
wits and my digestion have been my sole weapons
during life ; and I flatter myself I have never
used them otherwise than with consideration." ..

Mildred stared at him in genuine astonish-
ment. It was quite evident that he believed
what he was saying. He caught the look.

" I have never been cruel. Cruelty revolts
me. I once nearly killed a fellow in the streets
of Jo'burg for ill-treating a pony. Do you
remember ? "

" Yes, I remember."

" Have I ever been cruel to you, Milly ?
Did I ever raise a finger to you, or speak a rough
word to you during the whole of our married
life ? "

" No. But you worked night and day, all
the same, to break my spirit. You failed,
though ! "

Cradock nodded.

" I certainly did. You're as hard as nails.
However, we are wasting time. Talking of
nails, let us get down to brass tacks. How are
you situated here ? Well off ? Still in possession of that snugly invested little fortune that
you always insisted I married you for ? " He
was standing up now, smiling down upon her,
a mendicant unconcealed and unashamed.

" We have sufficient, thank you."

" I mean, are you in a position to support a husband ? " With a comprehensive gesture he indicated the comfortable appointments of Abbot's Mill. " It looks like it. Very well, then. Ulysses has come home—to spend his declining years with Penelope and Telemachus. I forget if Ulysses had a daughter. Or if you prefer it, the prodigal has returned. Serve the veal ! "

With his hands in his pockets, he strolled up to the window, stretched himself luxuriously, and gazed contentedly out into the sunny garden. This done, he turned to find his wife standing behind him.

" You can't stay here," she said.

Cradock extended a deprecating hand.

" I was expecting that. But listen to me. The whole matter can be adjusted quite simply. Why not acknowledge me as your miraculously restored husband, who lost his memory owing to exposure in the wreck, and has just found it —and you—again ? What a romance ! What a thrill for the neighbourhood ! Why can't I stay ? I do so long to stay." His voice dropped to a soothing, caressing murmur, which Mildred, among other women, knew well. " Why can't we settle down to a real Indian summer together ? I would make amends. Word of honour, Milly ! "

There were tears in his eyes. For the moment he was profoundly convinced that he was speaking the truth. But Mildred knew her man.

" You are going away from here," she said rigidly, " and never coming back."

In a moment Cradock's attack of sentiment had passed. He put his hands back in his pockets, smiled whimsically, and inquired :

" Is it permitted to ask why ? "

" Certainly. Because I have brought up my children to believe that their father was a decent man."

" Then why not let them go on believing it ? "

" I intend them to. That is why you are going away, my friend."

Cradock made a wry face.

" *Touché !* " he said.

" Do you think," cried Mildred, turning on him suddenly, " that you could live in the same house with them for a week and not be found out ? "

" I flatter myself that I could. I can be rather engaging when I like. You know that, Milly."

" God pity me, I do ! But that feeling has been dead in me for more than fifteen years. If need be, I shall have you turned out of the house."

Cradock smiled indulgently.

" It can't be done," he said. " You can't
have your lawful husband thrown out of his
own house."

" Lawful ?   The law can release me from you
to-morrow—and   shall ! "

" No, it won't !   You won't ask it to."

" Why not ? "

" Pride !   Pride !   Pride !   What would the
Smiths and the Browns say ?   What would the
Robinsons say ?   What would Laura Meakin
say ?   Ah, that gets home !   You see, I have
been making inquiries about you, Milly.   You
are highly respected here ;   this pleasant house
is the social centre of the neighbourhood.   You
won't sacrifice all that, for the sake—— "

" *Can't*   you understand ? "   blazed Mildred.
" I'm a mother !   I'll sacrifice everything—life
itself—yours   or   mine—or   both—to   rid   my
children of the contamination of your presence ! "

Cradock whistled long and softly.   A new
avenue of attack had providentially revealed
itself to him.

" Oh ! "   he said ;   " the children ?   They are
your hostages to fortune—eh ?   But think a
moment,   Milly !   They're my children   too ;
they may take my side.   Joan, for instance.
Joan must be almost a woman by this time ;
and a woman always has a soft spot for—a
soldier of fortune."

"Joan is my daughter," retorted Mildred hotly, "and therefore no fool. All she needs from me is a warning. All I needed twenty-two years ago was a warning—only there was no one to give it to me!"

"Well, our dear son, then? He might sympathise with my propensities. Like father, like son, you know!"

This time he had spoken the truth, and Mildred knew it. Realisation of that fact appeared in her eyes—and real terror.

"Never! Never! Never!" she cried.

Cradock heaved a gentle sigh of relief. He was on solid ground at last.

"Don't make a scene, Milly," he said soothingly "there's a good girl! You know I hate scenes. Listen to me. I'm not the sort of fellow to put any woman in a tight corner. We can settle this little matter in two minutes, in one of two ways. Either you can announce to the family that Father has come home, and we can all settle down and live happily ever after; or else, if you are ashamed of poor old broken-down me—after all, I might prove a drag upon your social ambitions—why not introduce me as Captain Conway, who has returned from South Africa after twenty years, and has unexpectedly run across you, the wife of his old friend Cradock, in this quiet little up-river resort? I stay on for a little while

as your guest; I find the locality delightful;
I decide to settle here; I take a little house
close by. (Of course, *you* take it really; but
I would never give a lady away.) I mingle with
the local nobility and gentry and beauty and
fashion, as your little protégé. There must be
some very jolly week-end parties in some of
these big places round here. I wonder if they
play bridge at all. Possibly one might get a
little baccarat, too, or chemmy. In that way
I could make a humble but honest living,
supplemented by an occasional fiver from you,
and at the same time gratify my paternal
yearnings—from a respectable distance, of course!
There, what do you say to that? The bargain
is in your favour; but I never could haggle!
Think it over!"

During this characteristic harangue Mildred
stood by the open window, staring stonily out
over the lawn towards the river, with her back
to the orator. Suddenly she was conscious of
young, limber, white-clad figures upon the little
jetty, busy about the launch. A shout of
laughter came floating across the lawn:
probably Leo was delivering a disquisition
upon the internal combustion engine. Then
Joan and Denny detached themselves from the
group, and came strolling across the grass
towards the house.

In a flash Mildred's course was made plain, and her mind made up. But time pressed; the pair were only fifty yards away. She whirled round upon her husband and cut him short.

"Listen to me!" she said, speaking in a low, rapid voice. "I believe in God, and I say my prayers to Him every night and every morning. Every morning I thank Him for my children, and every night I thank Him again for them; and after that I thank Him for having removed them from your influence just at a moment in their lives when you were beginning to be really poisonous to them. Well, God has sent you back to me! I don't know why, but I suppose there's a reason. All I know is that God can't possibly mean you to stay with us; but for the present I can't see my way out. I'm groping in sudden darkness. But one thing has been made clear to me—as clear as daylight. The children must never know that you are their father. Thank you for warning me of that!"

"Oh, I warned you, did I?" Cradock was plainly a little taken aback.

"Yes. You said, 'Like father, like son!' That's just it! It's Denny I'm thinking about —Denny! He's weak, horribly weak; but so far he's not vicious. His great standby so far has been his belief that his father was a decent sort of man—and that he takes after his father. If I acknowledge you as his father, if he gets to know the sort of person his father is—as he would in no time—his chief prop and stay will be withdrawn from him, and he'll give up trying! He'll go the same way as you! And to save him from that I'll fight till I drop! So I accept your second alternative—until I see my way clear to getting rid of you altogether. I don't know how I'm going to do it ; I haven't been able to think yet. But I'll do it. In the last extremity I could kill you—and I wouldn't hesitate to do so! So—don't drive me too far ! "

Denis Cradock gaped. He had always known his wife, beneath her placid breeding, for a woman of spirit, but this tigress was a sheer revelation to him. For the moment he was fairly cowed. He tried to speak, but failed.

An eager and aggrieved voice broke the silence.

" Mum, what on earth are you doing ? We've been waiting hours and hours. Oh, I beg your pardon ! "

Joan, half-way into the room, caught sight of the stranger, and recoiled precipitately on to her brother's toes.

" Come in, children ! " said Mildred, smiling. " I have a real surprise for you. This is Captain Conway, whom I haven't seen since the

South African days. He is just home, and ran across us quite by accident. Come and shake hands."

Joan was presented first. Captain Conway took her hand affably.

"I know you, Joan," he said, "but you don't know me."

Joan vouchsafed no answer, but after the fashion of her sex—which can never be comfortably neutral about its fellow-creatures—conceived an instant and permanent dislike for the visitor.

"And this, I suppose," said Conway, releasing Joan's hand, "is Denny?"

Father and son shook hands. They were much of a height, and surveyed one another with mutual interest. Conway turned to Mildred.

"He reminds me so much of his father," he said.

Denny broke in eagerly.

"Did you know my father well, sir?"

Conway laughed.

"None better!" he said.

"Oh, I say!" Denny, genuinely thrilled, shook Conway's hand again. Joan, muttering something about "more Ancestor Worship," subsided resignedly upon the sofa.

"Please, sir, is your fly to wait? Because——" Simmons was standing in the doorway.

Conway threw back his handsome head and laughed—a hearty, infectious laugh.

"Bless me!" he cried; "I had forgotten all about that fly! There's extravagance for you!"

"You must stay and spend the day with us, Captain Conway," interposed Mildred readily. "Send the fly away."

"Now, that's what I call real Old Country hospitality!" exclaimed the returned exile. "I shall be delighted. Did the cabman say how much?"

"He said three-and-six, sir," replied Simmons.

"I wonder if I have any silver about me," said Conway, feeling in his pockets. "I don't believe I have. I've got a fiver somewhere, I know. I wonder if—— ?"

He turned apologetically to his hostess.

Mildred bit her lip. Here was a foretaste of coming events. But Denny produced a ten-shilling note in a flash.

"Here you are, sir," he said, "if that's any use."

"Thank you, Denny," said Conway, taking it. "Now don't forget to remind me about this." He handed the note to Simmons. "Tell the man he can keep the change." Then he slipped his arm affectionately into the arm of his only son.

"What about that picnic we've all been hearing so much about?" he demanded boisterously. "The jolly old river again—eh! I feel a new man!"

RIPLEIGH REGATTA is one of the pleasantest of
the up-river festivals. It is not an aquatic
circus, like Henley; neither is it swamped by a
too convenient train service from Town, as at
Maidenhead; yet it is not so remote or so
obscure as to be disregarded by the metropolitan
and university crews. The Ripleigh Grand
Challenge Cup is a valuable prize. Last year
it was won by Jesus College, Cambridge, after
a memorable struggle with Thames Rowing
Club, New College and London having gone
down gloriously in the semi-final. Altogether
Ripleigh Regatta is not an event to be taken
lightly, I can assure you.

Denny Cradock and Leo Bagby were not
particularly interested in the fate of the Grand
Challenge Cup. Their field of vision was entirely
occupied by the Darnborough Vase, an unsightly
receptacle of silver gilt, the prospective property
for twelve months of the crew who should win
the Junior-Senior Fours. The Ripleigh Four,
the local hope, consisting of Denny at stroke and
Leo at three, with a stout pair of brothers named

Bullock at bow and two, had been training hard
for nearly three weeks. Each evening they put
forth in their frail craft ; and with a youth at the
helm, in the person of Master Bobby Devereux,
lent by the Vicarage, proceeded to row courses,
half courses, minutes, half minutes, and short
bursts, after the accepted canons of amateur
rowing (which have not changed a particle
since sliding seats were invented) until now,
upon the eve of the Regatta, they found themselves as physically fit and mechanically perfect
as plain living and high endeavour could make
them.

Their chief difficulty had been to secure
adequate coaching. A good rowing coach is
a pearl of great price—and corresponding
rarity. He must be able not only to point
out to the oarsman the errors of his way, but
to tell him what to do to correct them—a rare
combination in any critic. He must also possess
an authoritative manner and lungs of brass.
Under these conditions an asthmatic and intermittent vicar on a bicycle can only be described
as a *pis aller*.

Great, then, was the joy of the Ripleigh
Junior-Senior crew when the heavens opened,
and Captain Dale Conway—soldier, athlete,
and very engaging man of the world—descended
therefrom and volunteered to coach them. His

offer was accepted with acclamation, and the crew made marked progress from that hour. Captain Conway was perhaps not quite such a good coach as he sounded; but, as a popular preacher once observed in a confiding moment: "It's the air of conviction that does it." At any rate Conway succeeded in animating his charges with complete belief in their own invulnerability, which is the only thing that really matters in racing—or indeed in most phases of the battle of life.

It was six o'clock on the evening before the Regatta, and the crew were returning from their final practice in a quiet part of the river. They had just eased after a short burst, and now sat humped over their oars, panting contentedly and paying respectful attention to the words of their preceptor, who reclined gracefully against a bicycle upon the towpath.

"Very well rowed! Much better all round; but you're still inclined to rush the first few strokes. Remember it's no use swinging right out for the second stroke—or the third, for that matter. Keep your slides right back, and content yourselves with getting a quick grip of the water. When the boat has really begun to run, you can swing till your noses hit the keel, if you like. It shouldn't be difficult: there's a strong stream running after all the rain we've

had. Bow, keep your hands up over the
stretcher, or you'll be late on Three all the
time. Three's a big, bouncing boy, I know,
but that's no reason why he should row one
side of the boat along all by himself. Cox,
watch Bow's blade, and give him ginger every
time he's late. Stroke, old man, you have still
got a dirty finish. The only way to cure it is
by getting a harder beginning; so steady
forward! Now, everybody, we'll try one more
start, and see if we can't get her off like a stone
out of a catapult. Remember there's only one
rule in boat-racing, and that is to get the lead
and stick to it. Get forward!—I want to see
ten strokes in the first quarter of a minute this
time—are you ready? Row . . . . Oh, well
done, well done! Easy, Cox!"

On the opposite side of the river, moored to
the bank, lay a punt containing Joan and Uncle
Tony.

"They certainly have come on a lot since he
took them in hand," remarked Joan, gazing
across the river. "Do you think he's really
any good as a coach, Uncle Tony?"

Sir Anthony surveyed his critical young companion quizzically.

"That sounds as if you didn't, Joan."

"You're right I don't see how such a born

humbug could really be much good at anything,"
replied Joan, with characteristic candour.

Uncle Tony removed his pipe from his mouth,
leaned forward, and extended a hand.

" Shake ! " he said.

Joan complied, and, the Anti-Conway Lodge
being thus formally inaugurated, the pair
resumed their positions at opposite ends of
the punt and smiled at one another—the rare
smile of those fortunate people who can understand without explanations.

" He's an interesting rascal," said Uncle Tony
thoughtfully—" a curious case. I have been
studying him pretty closely for the past three
weeks. He seems to be entirely devoid of
moral principle and utterly without compassion
or conscience of any kind ; yet one cannot
deny that he is a genial, breezy, attractive
fellow, and a delightful companion when he likes.
Am I right in supposing that he has brought his
talents to bear on you already, Joan ? "

" Oh, yes. He began the day after he arrived."

" What line did he take ? "

" He began by working the ' old-friend-of-
your-father ' act."

" To which, I suppose, you retaliated with a
few observations on Ancestor Worship ? "

" I believe I did."

" That choked him off, I'll be bound."

" Oh dear, no. One evening last week he took me out on the river in a punt. He tied the punt to a willow stump, and told me the sad story of his life."

" Poor fellow ! What made it sad ? "

" His wife. He had been married."

" I can believe that, without any difficulty whatsoever. She didn't understand him, of course ? "

" You've hit it. She set his own children against him, too—— "

" That hardly sounds necessary."

" ——And finally he lost her."

" That should not have been so difficult. Is she dead ? "

Joan gave a little gurgle of laughter.

" That's what I asked," she said. " Apparently I shouldn't have. I knew I'd made a *faux pas* the moment I'd spoken."

" It was most tactless of you," remarked Uncle Tony severely. " You pinned him down to a plain statement of fact—yea or nay ? No wonder he was pained. What did he say ? "

" He buried his face in his hands—like this— and gave a sort of groan, and then asked me to spare him ! "

" That means, ' Give me time to think of a good one ! ' What did he say when he had recovered ? "

" He said," replied Joan with relish, " that life was a desert, and I was an oasis."

" Very pretty. And how did you react to that piece of information ? "

" I said I didn't think I was green enough to be an oasis."

This time Uncle Tony leaned back and laughed out loud.

" You're an unsentimental young woman, Joan," he said ; " but you've got your head screwed on the right way."

Joan did not reply. She was watching the boat, now far downstream, indulging in a final burst before putting into port.

" They did ten strokes all right that time," she said with approval. " Has he tried to get round you at all, Uncle Tony ? "

" Not yet. Probably he is reserving me as a forlorn hope. How does he get on with the rest of the family ? "

Joan's brow puckered.

" He's after both Denny and Leo, I'm afraid. Of course Leo's quite safe."

Uncle Tony looked genuinely surprised.

" You don't say so ! " he said.

" Yes. If Leo gets into a mess, he'll come and tell me about it," explained Joan with composure, " and I'll get him out of it."

" I was forgetting," said Sir Anthony gravely,
Then he added :

" Do you love that boy, Joan ? "

Joan reddened. As her mother had noted,
she was utterly reticent about her own
heart.

" He's a great big helpless baby," she said ;
" and I'd give—everything—to save him from
hurting himself."

" O fortunate youth ! " murmured Uncle Tony
softly. " Proceed, my dear ! "

" Denny is the difficulty," said Joan, in a
troubled voice. " He is self-conscious, and that
makes him secretive. I'm sorry for people like
that : they are so sensitive that sometimes they
simply can't go straightforward. When Denny
was quite a little boy, he was always playing his
own games, and having his own pretends ; and
he was so afraid of being criticised or laughed at
that very often he got into a row for concealing
something, or denying something, that was
perfectly harmless really."

" You appear to have some knowledge of
human nature, Joan."

" I suppose I have, in some ways. I wonder
where I get it from. Not mother : she is a
child at judging character. My late papa,
perhaps. One thing I am thankful for, and that
is that Molly isn't at home. She would simply

have wallowed in dear Captain Conway—almost
as badly as Mother."

" Ha ! " said Anthony, looking up. " Is
Mother wallowing ? "

" I should think she was. Haven't you
noticed ? "

" I am afraid I have, Joan. Conway is just
the type to influence your mother. The kinder
and gentler a woman is, the more easily she
succumbs to the Conways of this world."

Joan smiled impishly.

" Laura Meakin has made up her mind
differently," she said.

" Ah, the lady who is going to hold a meeting
in your mother's drawing-room to-morrow ?
What of her ? "

" She has decided that if there is any suc-
cumbing to be done in this neighbourhood she'll
do it herself. The silly creature's in love with
him. What's more, she thinks Mother is too ;
and she's as jealous—— "

Sir Anthony glanced at Joan keenly.

" Your mother—eh ? Is that true, Joan ? "

Joan clasped her hands in unwonted agitation.

" Uncle Tony," she said, " I don't know ! I
don't know ! It seems absurd even to consider
such a thing being possible—Mother making a
fool of herself over a man at her time of life.
But—well, there it is ! What do you think ? "

" Tell me what you think.   Your sex possesses
certain exasperating but invaluable intuitions,
denied to mere man."

For a moment Joan sat with her hands clasped
round her knees, gazing downstream towards
the raft, where the four boys had just hoisted
their frail craft from the water preparatory to
carrying it into the boat-house. Master Bobby
Devereaux, clinging manfully to the switching
tail of the vessel, was, as usual, nearly flicked
into the river by his playful companions ; and
a shout of laughter came floating upstream
Then Joan spoke again.

" Uncle Tony, there is something queer going
on at home : I can feel it whenever Captain
Conway comes into the house. He has some
influence over Mother. It may be love ; it
may be fear ; but she does whatever he tells
her. She doesn't seem to want to see him,
yet she does see him. He's in and out of the
place all day long. What's more, she goes and
visits him."

" God bless me ! At his bungalow ? "

" Yes."

" That's very imprudent ? "

" Imprudent ? It's insane ! Why, Laura
Meakin saw her three days ago, coming out."

" And Laura has been—broadcasting—eh ? "

" I should think she has. ' She says it very

loud and clear ; she says it in the Vicar's ear,' "
quoted Joan.

" What is impelling your mother to do this ?
Love, or fear ? "

Joan regarded her uncle steadily for a moment,
then spoke. She was not a girl who evaded
realities.

" I hate to say it, but something tells me it's
love."

Uncle Tony shook his head.

" I respect your instincts, Joan, but I don't
agree with you. My theory is that this man
has some hold over your mother—some secret
or other."

" But, Uncle Tony, can you imagine Mother
ever having done anything shady in her life !
The whole thing would be funny, if it weren't
so tragic."

Uncle Tony sat up, and knocked the ashes
out of his pipe.

" That's the word, Joan," he said—" ' tragic.'
There's a black spirit of tragedy hovering over
this little backwater of ours : one can almost
hear its ghostly wings rustling. In these
surroundings the whole thing seems ludicrous.
We row, we picnic, we frivol ; we haven't a
care in the world ! But the Spirit is there,
waiting to pounce. Joan, we must exorcise
that Spirit."

" But how ? Surely Mother, of all people, can't have done anything that this man could use against her ? "

" I am quite sure she hasn't. But perhaps someone else has."

" Who ? "

" That remains to be seen. It is not always for our own actions that we have to suffer. But I'll talk to your mother."

" I wish you would. Now we must get home to dinner, or there'll be a yowl from the boys."

Joan took the pole and began to propel the punt downstream with her long, easy swing.

" I imagine Captain Conway will also be present at the meal," said Sir Anthony.

" No great stretch of imagination is required," replied Joan. " By the way, I wonder if Thwaites knows anything about him."

" Who is Thwaites ? "

" That grim-faced lady who has taken the place of the late lamented Simmons. She was Mother's maid for years. She left us to do war-work ; and now she's come back. I'll pump her, but I don't suppose I shall get much change out of her. She's as close as an oyster Mind that willow-branch ! "

THE soi-disant Dale Conway strolled along the crowded towpath, recognising acquaintances, returning salutations, and basking in the grateful sunshine of social popularity. He had only been in Ripleigh for three weeks, but already that exclusive stronghold of nice people was his to play upon as he would.

It was Regatta Day, and the time was a quarter past four. The final for the Darnborough Vase was to be rowed at four-fifty; and the Ripleigh Junior-Senior Crew, having drawn a bye in the first round and defeated a London four in the second, were to participate therein. Conway had just left them, sitting in a row upon their raft, and whistling forlornly through chattering teeth. Even his optimistic and vivid forecast of the result of the race had been insufficient to eradicate the symptoms of that distressing malady known as " the needle."

However, nerves usually vanish when the time for action comes. At this moment the crew swung past him on their way to the starting post, sitting their boat nicely and evoking a

H

patriotic and well-merited cheer from the Ripleigh spectators. Cradock politely elbowed his way to the edge of the stream for a better view. At his feet, moored to the towpath, lay a punt. His eye fell upon the occupants. The first was a small man with a peaky face and a disillusioned expression. He was wearing a suit of what is usually known as sponge-bag check, and a panama hat. He was accompanied in the punt by a henna-haired lady of about his own age, who looked like the mother of all barmaids, and two ravishing young creatures—one blonde and the other brunette— with cheeks of exactly the same shade of pink and vermilion mouths of precisely the same shape.

Cradock reached down and tapped the small man upon the shoulder.

" Good afternoon, Moon ! " he said.

Mr. Moon jumped ; apparently being tapped upon the shoulder awoke disturbing memories. Then he turned cautiously, and came face to face with his late employer.

Cradock gave an almost imperceptible jerk of his head, and turned on his heel and disappeared into the crowd. Mr. Moon extracted himself painfully from the punt and followed him, in his usual dejected fashion.

Presently the pair foregathered in a quiet

spot behind a refreshment tent. Cradock shook hands affably.

" You got home from America all right ? " he inquired.

" Yes, sir. Not for a bit, though. I had to keep on moving round the country for more than a year after I left you, on account of what they called the Selective Draft. However, I got back in the end."

" Good ! What's your game now ? "

Mr. Moon flinched.

" No game at all, sir, I assure you. We're straight—more or less."

Cradock surveyed him thoughtfully. He was not the man to let slip such instruments as Providence placed in his hand.

" Are you under police supervision at present ? " he asked.

" Oh no, sir ! "

" However, I suppose there are certain little episodes of the past which, if they did come to light, might make your position an extremely delicate one ? "

" They would make it something chronic," said Mr. Moon frankly.

" Well, I won't give you away to anybody."

" Thank you, sir "

" Still, one good turn deserves another. Perhaps you can help me." Mr. Moon flinched again. " What do you do for a living now ? "

" Well, Lizzie is running a Dancing Academy
in Maida Vale."

" Lizzie ? "

" Yes, sir ; the wife."

" The lady in the punt—the elder lady ? "

" Yes, sir. She had a hard time when I was
abroad, and she's none too strong now. 'Er
valves—— "

" Go and fetch her."

Mr. Moon shambled away, and Cradock,
having lit a cigarette, devoted the ensuing
three minutes to reflection. His resourceful
imagination had already included the Moon
ménage in the cast of a little drama which he
proposed shortly to stage in Ripleigh.

Next moment Mrs. Moon stood before him,
deferential and overheated, and was duly
presented by her husband.

" I hear you conduct a Dancing Academy,
Mrs. Moon," said Cradock.

" Yes, sir. Ballroom and stage dancing.
Private lessons."

" And what are Mr. Moon's precise duties
in the establishment ? Don't tell me that he
is one of your instructors ! "

" Oh no, sir," interposed Moon, plainly a
little shocked at the suggestion. " I do a bit
on the side."

" On the same premises as the Dancing Academy ? "

" Yes, sir. I run a baccarat table of an evening—for a few select ladies and gents."

" Are you doing anything in the turf line at present ? "

" Very little, sir."

" Well, never mind. Now, listen to me ! You see that house down there, above the lock ? It's called Abbot's Mill."

" Yes, sir."

" Well, I want you and Mrs. Moon to come there this evening at a quarter past six. There's to be a large meeting held in the drawing-room, in aid of some object which I have forgotten. Admission is free, so don't be afraid to walk right in. You will find me occupying the distinguished post of Chairman. Don't be surprised if I mention your name. I may propose you for an office of some kind, but your duties will be purely nominal and honorary ; so don't offer any opposition, whatever you do. By the way, who are the girls in the punt, Mrs. Moon ? Your daughters ? "

" No, sir. We never had—— "

" Well, who are they ? "

" Two of our dancing instructresses, sir. Miss Gladys Arbuthnot and—— "

" Are they nice girls ? "

" Very nice, sir."

" Refined," added Mr. Moon.

" What are they doing at a regatta ? "

" Well, sir, they sometimes come across some of our gentlemen clients, and sit about with them—in punts——"

" That's right," corroborated Mr. Moon. " Under trees."

" And they introduce their friends to Gus, with a view to the baccarat business."

" I understand. I think you had better not bring them to the meeting, though I may want them later. You are staying for the fireworks, of course ? "

" If you wish it, sir."

" Very good. Buzz off, now. You can all come on to my bungalow after the meeting— the girls too. I know a couple of young gentlemen who would be only too pleased to shake a cocktail for them. By Jove, there's the race coming over ! "

And Cradock, precipitately abandoning the Moons, ran frantically to the towpath, just in time to see Denny and his crew sweep gallantly past the post, victorious by half a length.

CAPTAIN DALE CONWAY rose to his feet, amid applause from the crowded little drawing-room —or rather, drawing and breakfast-room made one by throwing open the double doors between. The applause was led by Denny and Leo, who, flushed with triumph in the matter of the Darnborough Vase, were inclined to be boisterously tolerant of everything in general— even the activities of Laura Meakin.

" May I sum up for you very briefly," he suggested, " the results of this meeting—this admirably organised meeting ? " He bowed gallantly to Laura, who bridled consciously. " Before doing so, though, I must thank you on Miss Meakin's behalf for the very practical manner in which you have expressed your sympathy, by your attendance here this after-noon, with the aims "—he glanced covertly at the agenda paper on the table before him— " of The League of Educative Science."

" Tea, really," observed Joan, in a painfully audible undertone.

" And," continued the speaker, " may I also

take this opportunity of expressing my personal
sense of the honour you have done me in
appointing me your Chairman ? As I stand here in
the presence of that Elder Statesman, that retired
Proconsul of our Eastern Empire, Sir Anthony
Fenwick, I am painfully conscious that he and
not I ought to be occupying that position."

" Hear, hear ! " cried Denny and Leo cordially.

There was much laughter at this, in which
Cradock joined.

" Anyhow, here I am," he said, " and I hope
I have not made an utter mess of things."

" Rather ! " said the indefatigable Leo.

" Order ! " cried Laura Meakin, in a deep voice.

" But you have not only made me Chairman
of this meeting; you have appointed me
Treasurer of your Society as well—a mark of
confidence which moves me very deeply. I
know, of course, that that confidence is derived,
in great measure, from the affection and esteem
in which you hold my very dear friend and
sponsor, our hostess of this afternoon—— "

The applause this time was quite spontaneous.
Mildred, sitting alone, a little apart from the
table, bowed her head, presumably in modest
gratification.

" Still," continued the Chairman, " sentiment
is one thing and business is another. Let me
say, here and now, that I will not and cannot

accept this responsible post unless the accounts
of the Society are regularly and properly audited
by an outside authority."

" Hear, hear ! " remarked Sir Anthony, who
was acting as corner-man at the left end of
the front row.   Cradock bowed in his direction.

" I am glad to be supported in my contention
by so eminent an authority," he said.   " Fortunately, we have not far to go for our auditor.
By the greatest good fortune Mr. Augustus
Moon, of the widely-known firm of Chartered
Accountants of that name in Lincoln's Inn
Fields, Messrs. Moon, Moon & Moon, happens to
be present in our midst this afternoon.   As an old
rowing man he has been lured here by the Regatta,
in company with Mrs. Moon, whom I know we
are delighted to welcome among us——"

He paused, significantly, but there was no
response.   It was clear that Mr. Moon's name
was not quite so well known in Ripleigh as in
Lincoln's Inn Fields.

" Go on, you fool ! " hissed Leo to Denny.
" Clap ! "

" Oh, sorry ! " said Denny ; and the pair
applauded lustily, with the respectful assistance
of the rest of the company, now awakened to
a tardy sense of the honour which Mr. Moon's
presence conferred.

" Mr. Moon," explained Cradock, " has kindly
H*

undertaken to examine the accounts of the Society without charge of any kind, both now and at any other date that may be necessary; and I am sure we are all most proud and grateful to possess such a distinguished Honorary Auditor." He bowed in the direction of a twitching figure in a distant corner. "Mr. Moon, on behalf of the members of the Society, I thank you!"

The audience, now quite carried away by the nobility of Mr. Moon's conduct, broke into prolonged applause. Mr. Moon promptly lost his head. He rose to his feet.

" Mr. Chairman, Ladies, Gentlemen, and fellersports—— " he began.

Mr. Chairman had not quite bargained for this.

" In a minute, Mr. Moon," he said smoothly, with an almost imperceptible glance towards Mrs. Moon. An iron hand in a hot kid glove promptly drew Mr. Moon down into his seat, and the formal business of the meeting was resumed.

" The sums actually handed in to date," announced Cradock, consulting a paper of figures handed to him by Laura Meakin, " amount to eighty-seven pounds, eleven shillings and fourpence. A very encouraging total! But "—his voice rose firmly above a gentle murmur of gratification—" it has one feature to which I object. It is not a round sum. Now, I have a little suggestion to make. I

am going to ask Miss Meakin to hand all these
cheques and postal orders to me, as a free gift,
to be my very own, to be sent to my bank and
placed to my private account." (*Mild sensation.*) "In return, I shall write a cheque for
one hundred pounds, and shall present it to
myself, as Treasurer, for the use of the Society.
If you will sanction my action you will be
getting rid of this tiresome, untidy tale of
shillings and pence, and at the same time
conferring a very real favour upon your chairman. May I do that, please?"

The audience, completely hypnotised by this
time, applauded frantically. But Cradock held
up a hand.

"Just one point," he said. "Let us be quite
frank. It is not always wise to accept cheques
from strangers."

"Hear, hear!" remarked an approving voice
from the corner seat.

"I am glad, Sir Anthony, that we again
see eye to eye," said Cradock, smiling. "Now,
I am a stranger. Yes, I am!"—this against
a faint murmur of dissent—"a comparative
stranger, anyhow! But Mrs. Cradock is no
stranger to you. You all know Mrs. Cradock.
I, too, know Mrs. Cradock. I have known her
for more years than her appearance would lead
you to believe——"

There was appreciative laughter, and Joan reddened angrily at the familiarity.

"So I am going to ask Mrs. Cradock, when I draw my cheque for the hundred pounds, to write her name on the back of it ; and I venture to think that such an endorsement will make that cheque as good as a Bank of England note." He turned with an eloquent gesture to his hostess. "Mrs. Cradock, will you do that ? "

Mildred, helpless but composed, bowed her head, amid more hand-clapping.

"Thank you ! " cried Cradock enthusiastically. "I knew you would ! Now I think we might disperse. I know one or two gentlemen who have to go and collect Regatta prizes. Is there any other business ? "

There was none, except a laborious vote of thanks to the chair, proposed by Sir Thomas Mobberley, the local M.P. ; seconded by Leo Bagby, who contrived with great presence of mind to cut in during one of the proposer's portentous pauses ; and carried by acclamation, before Sir Thomas, or his life-long prompter, Lady Mobberley, had time to realise what was happening. After that came a general up-heaval, and the meeting streamed out of the open windows on to the lawn. Foremost in the retreat one might have observed the hurrying figures of Mr. and Mrs. Augustus Moon.

PRESENTLY Cradock found himself alone with Laura Meakin, gathering up loose threads of business.

" One or two of these cheques are made payable to you, Miss Meakin," he said. " Would you kindly endorse them ? "

" With pleasure, Captain Conway," replied Laura. " You and I are transacting quite a lot of business together these days, aren't we ? " she added archly.

Cradock looked up and smiled.

" The worst of transacting business with a girl like you, Miss Meakin," he said, " is that I find it increasingly difficult to concentrate my mind upon the business."

" Now you're being naughty," announced Laura, and dealt him a disabling tap upon the wrist with a fountain pen. " I don't think I shall ask you to tea with me, to-morrow."

Captain was all repentance at once.

" Please ! I was carried away for the moment."

" You promise to be good, then ? "

" Faithfully."

" Very well. Come about five."

" Right. By the way, I think I can get those oil shares for you, after all, and on very favourable terms, too. However, we can discuss that to-morrow. Here is our hostess."

Mildred stood in the open window, hospitably solicitous.

" Laura, dear," she said, " I have just ordered some fresh tea for you."

Laura rose and replied, a trifle testily :

" Thank you, Mildred, but I only drink China tea. I shall go home and make my own. Good-bye ! " She kissed her hostess frigidly. " You are looking ten years more than your age to-day. What Captain Conway said about you in his speech was only flattery ; you mustn't believe things like that. I thought I ought to tell you."

" Thank you for not forgetting, dear," said Mildred meekly.

Laura shook hands heavily with her chairman.

" Good-bye, Captain Conway," she said. " You won't forget about to-morrow ? "

" Is it likely ? " Without a tremor Cradock kissed Laura's black kid glove, and Laura, with a conscious glance in the direction of her rival strode out of the window and was no more seen.

Cradock chuckled and turned to his wife.

" Now, Milly—— " he began.

Mildred interrupted him. Laura had been right : she did look ten years more than her age.

" Denis," she said hotly, " this sort of thing can't go on any longer."

" You're quite right, my dear ; it can't. I have a proposal to make to you which will regularise the situation completely."

" What have you to say now that you couldn't have said any time during these three weeks ? "

" This. The situation has developed ; a new state of things has arisen. I want to—— "

There was a step on the gravel outside, and Master Denny appeared in the window, smoking like a furnace.

" Oh, Denny, my dear boy, what a big pipe ! " exclaimed Mildred, obviously grateful for his appearance.

" Yes, Mum," replied her son complacently, " the biggest I've got. Furthermore and in addition, I have just drunk the longest drink I ever drank, and to-night I am going to eat the biggest dinner I ever ate ; after which I shall really feel that I am out of training. Hallo, Conway ! Congratters on your chairmanship ! "

Then, unobservant though he was, Denny caught the look on his mother's face.

" I say, Mum," he exclaimed, " you're looking all in. It's that rotten pow-wow of Laura's. Let me take you on the river for half an hour."

" I have rather a head, dear," said Mildred. " I think I'll go upstairs and rest."

" Righto ! Take my arm. Don't go away, Conway ; I shall be back directly."

Denny disappeared up the stairs with his mother's arm in his. Cradock stood fast, cogitating.

The swing door opened, and the successor of Simmons, the implacable Thwaites, stood before him, bearing a newly-charged teapot. She favoured her late employer with a truculent glare, and addressed him.

" Well, I suppose you think you are the clever one ? "

" Moderately so, thank you, Thwaites."

" Don't be too proud of yourself, that's all. Remember, the only reason I don't go straight round the corner and fetch a policeman to you is that she begged me not to."

" She did right, Thwaites. The gratification experienced by you in performing such a feat would hardly have been worth the scandal brought upon this eminently respectable house-hold. I fancy you will have to go on keeping your tongue between your teeth indefinitely. Knowing you as I do, you have my sympathy.

But we all have our troubles in this world, haven't we ? "

Thwaites glared anew.

" There's them watching you," she announced, " that's as sharp as you are—and sharper. One of these days you'll run past yourself, and then you'll be sorry ! "

Here Denny was heard descending the stairs three steps at a time, and Thwaites passed on into the garden like a reluctant thunder-cloud.

Denny greeted his hero enthusiastically.

" Conway, old man," he said, " I can't tell you how grateful we are to you for coaching us. We'd never have done it without you."

" That's all right, Denny. Forget it—like your training ! Come down to my bungalow and have a drink. No more rules and regulations now, eh ? "

" No, by gum ! "

" I want you to meet my old pal Moon, too. He's a character, I can tell you."

" He looks it ! "

" I have just been talking to him seriously about his appearance. I ask you, Denny, as a man of the world, if you were to meet Moon suddenly in the street, would you take him for what he is—an eminent chartered accountant, with an anticipatory interest in the next Honours List—or a race-course tout ? "

"A tout," replied Denny with the frankness of youth.

Cradock laughed. "I'll tell him you said that," he cried. "Come along and make his acquaintance. In any case, I want you to give him the once over before you consider his invitation."

"Invitation?" Denny was all intrigued at once. "That sounds mysterious."

"Oh, it's nothing. I happen to be going up to town to-morrow. I may have to run over to Paris later. Oddly enough, I find the Moons are going over, too, with a couple of their nieces—remarkably pretty girls."

"Are they here to-day?" asked Denny eagerly.

"They are. I invited Mrs. Moon to bring them along to my bungalow. Will you come and shake a cocktail for them?"

"Will I not?"

"I presume you don't mind meeting girls who enjoy an occasional cocktail?" said Cradock, pausing in the window with Denny's arm in his.

"I didn't know there were any others—that one met anywhere," replied the boy grandly. "I mean, don't you think, in the present year of grace a girl who doesn't like cocktails and admits it ought to be put in a convent? What?"

" You feel that girls ought to have *savoir faire*—eh ? "

" That's just what I do mean. Come along."

But Cradock still held back. He wished to play his final card.

" By the way, you're quite sure Mother wouldn't mind ? "

Denny flushed.

" My dear fellow," he said stiffly, " I—one— a man does as he thinks fit in these matters. Of course, if one lives at home, one has to—— "

Cradock caught him up quickly.

" Exactly," he said. " You've hit it, Denny. So long as a man lives at home he has to conform to the laws of the Medes and Persians, and dance attendance on his womankind—at the end of an apron string, so to speak." Denny flinched visibly. " But with all respect to my old friend, your charming mother, it's possible to overdo that sort of thing. In fact, it's grossly unfair. A man, a man of the world like you, is bound to feel his oats at times. He wants to kick up his heels and buck, doesn't he ? "

The pair stood face to face with sparkling eyes, suddenly and amazingly alike.

" You see, old chap," said Cradock. " I understand ! "

" By God, you do ! "

"Then   why   not   take   a   fortnight   off   and
come   with   us ? "

"To   Paris ? "

"Paris—Deauville—anywhere you like.   Could
you   stand   old   Moon,   do   you   think ?   We'll get
him   some   new   clothes.   You'll   be   my   guest,   of
course.   I've   had   a   bit   of   luck   lately   on   the
turf."

This   was   indirectly   true.   Master   Leo   Bagby
had   recently   entrusted   his   mentor   with   a   considerable   cheque,   for   purposes   of   turf   specula-
tion—a   "system,"   Cradock   had   called   it—and
the cheque was   now burning a   hole in Cradock's
pocket.   He   pressed   his   advantage.

"It   will   be   a   glorious   party,"   he   said.   "You,
I,   Moon,   the   two   girls,   and   Mrs.   Moon   for
chaperon.   Give   this   dead   old   backwater   a   miss
for   a   bit,   Denny,   and   come   somewhere   with   me
where   you   can   splash   about   for   a   bit !   Come
where   there   is   life,   old   chap !   Life ! "

"I   must ! "   cried   Denny   ecstatically.   "I
must ! "

"That's   the   stuff,"   said   Cradock   approvingly.
"Come   along   to   the   bungalow   and   meet   the
girls,   for   a   start."

DENNY and Conway had searcely departed through the window when Sir Anthony entered in a manner distinctly furtive, by the door. In his hand he carried the evening paper. He stole to the sideboard, from which he extracted a sherry decanter and glass. He was engaged in filling one from the other when he heard a light step behind him. It was Joan.

"Hallo, Uncle Tony!" she said. "Proceeding from labour to refreshment?"

"Yes, my dear."

"What did you think of our chairman this afternoon?"

"He handled the meeting like a master. It may be an unpatriotic thing to say, but I do admire tact."

"What I admired chiefly was his cheek. Uncle Tony, where did he get his Honorary Auditor—and the Honorary Auditor's wife?"

"My dear, he told us. From the firm of Moon, Moon & Moon—or was it Moonshine? And he made the meeting swallow the Moons— all of them! I take off my hat to Conway, and I drink to his confusion!"

245

" I was talking to Thwaites this morning,''
said Joan, sitting down.

" Ah ! "

" But one might as well try to get blood out
of a stone. She simply closed up like a trap."

" That type of old servant," remarked Sir
Anthony, " would rather go to the stake than
betray a domestic secret. Our military friend
is quite safe so far as Thwaites is concerned, I
should say."

" You're right," said Joan. " Have you said
anything to Mother yet ? "

" No. I have had no opportunity."

" Well, I wish you would. I don't like the
way Captain Conway is getting Denny under
his thumb. So long as Denny was in training
for the races, things were all right ; but now—
with nothing to do—— "

" Satan finds some mischief still—and so on ?
Hallo, here is your mother coming downstairs."

" Then do it now ! " suggested practical
Joan. " I've promised to go on the river with
Leo."

She flitted through the open window, and
Sir Anthony rose to greet his niece.

" I was lying down upstairs," explained
Mildred, " and I heard your voices. I would
rather have your company than my own any
day, Uncle Tony," she added with her ready

smile. "Have the festivities of the afternoon exhausted you?"

"Which of them—the regatta or the meeting?"

"Whichever you please."

"The regatta exhausted me considerably—especially the gentleman with the black face and the prismatic trousers who cast anchor alongside our punt and sang 'Whose baby are you, dear?' into my left ear. But the meeting was a tonic. Our chairman is quite a character."

"You like him, then?"

"I find him most attractive—even though he referred to me in his speech as a retired Proconsul of our Eastern Empire."

"I suppose you have never met anyone quite like him before?" There was a note in Mildred's voice which implied that one has to make allowances for exceptional characters.

"Oh, yes, I have," said Uncle Tony unexpectedly. "There is a penal settlement in the Indian Ocean—to which I have frequently contributed recruits—full of people just like him—or as like him as they're able to be."

"What do you mean?" asked Mildred, fluttered.

"I mean, my dear," replied Sir Anthony deliberately, "that the man is an arrant scamp, and I shall make it my business to expose him."

Mildred turned to him in sudden fear.

" Uncle Tony, you mustn't ! "

" Why not ? "

" He's—he's—my friend ! "

" We don't always select our friends, Milly ;
sometimes we have to have them. Tell me, is
this man straight, or crooked ? "

" He's eccentric—impulsive. He—he does
foolish things at times. He has knocked about
the world ; he hasn't got our point of view.
Be patient with him, Uncle Tony ; I'll see he
doesn't do anything wrong. Only "—Mildred's
hands were clasped in unaccustomed entreaty—
" please, please don't try to find out anything
about him. If he were pressed too hard—— "

Sir Anthony regarded her curiously.

" You don't want him driven into a corner ? "

" No."

" For fear he might turn nasty ? "

" Yes."

" And expose somebody ? "

" Yes." A puzzled look crept into Mildred's
eyes.

" Not you—but *somebody*." Uncle Tony sat
down and took his niece's hand. " My dear,
brave, loyal Milly—— " he said.

There was real panic in Mildred's face now.

" Loyal ? " she whispered. " What do you
mean ? Have you guessed ? "

" I think so."

" What have you guessed ? "

" That in refusing to expose this man you are shielding someone else."

" Someone else ? "

" Or, rather, someone else's memory. Conway has found out something about your late husband and is blackmailing you."

Mildred gave a long, shuddering sigh. Sir Anthony was on a false scent. She did not know whether to be relieved on not.

" You are helpless," he continued, " because, if you fight, that precious record of which you are so proud—which you have taught your children to revere—might be smirched. Is that so ? "

Mildred bowed her head. This shrewd old man might be wrong in his premiss, but his conclusions were strangely near the truth.

" That is why I called you loyal," he said. " Now, can I help you ? "

" If only you could ! But you can't ! This has got to be my own private worry, and no one else's, Uncle Tony. We all have them ! " she smiled gallantly.

" There is one way," continued Sir Anthony " which I have seldom known to fail in these cases."

" What is that ? "

" To investigate his record, quietly.   I warrant
I'll find out something about him which will put
the boot on the other leg."

" No, no, no, no ! " exclaimed Mildred, with
a sudden return of her fears. " You mustn't
do that.   You will ruin everything if you do."

" I   shouldn't   publish   my   knowledge.   I
should just explain to him that I know who
he is—— "

" Uncle Tony," said Mildred earnestly, with
her hand on his arm—" don't ! You cannot
bring him down without bringing me down—
and the children too ! Don't ! "

The old man surveyed her gravely.

" It's as bad as that, is it ? " he said.   Mildred
nodded.   " Very well, then I won't.   But what's
to be done ? "

" You must have patience, dear Uncle Tony.
I have hopes of getting him to go away. I
have a plan : I think I can succeed. But
however you may feel, don't try to precipitate
things ! "

" Very well, my dear," said Sir Anthony,
rising : " we will keep our powder dry for the
present.   Meanwhile, whenever you want help,
remember that the battered old ruin who now
confronts you is entirely at your service."

" Bless you ! " said Mildred, kissing him.

Suddenly there came sounds of an altercation

outside the window. Two voices were audible —one loud, imperious, and passionately angry ; the other sulky and defiant. Mildred ran and looked out.

" What is it ? " asked Sir Anthony.

" Captain Conway, on the towpath."

" He appears to be reciting."

" He's talking to a rough-looking man—a man wheeling a Punch-and-Judy show."

" Doubtless another Honorary Auditor. Surely he's not going to bring *him* in ! "

" No, he's left him now. He's coming in here."

But before he entered the room Cradock whirled round and delivered himself of a final broadside in the direction of the towpath. Mildred watched him, half thrilled. Here, for the moment, was a different man—transfigured by generous indignation.

" And if I catch you at it again, you filthy swine," he shouted, " I'll chuck you into the river—and hold you under ! "

He turned contemptuously upon his heel, to find himself face to face with Mildred and Sir Anthony.

He smiled disarmingly.

" I beg your pardon," he said ; " I'm afraid I alarmed you. The fact is, that ruffian was knocking his dog about—the poor little Toby

brute that supports him. So—I knocked him
about! Idiotic, of course; but if there's one
thing in this world that revolts me, it's cruelty
of that kind."

"You are referring, I presume," said Sir
Anthony dryly, "to physical cruelty?"

"Is there any other kind that matters,"
snapped Cradock, "compared with that?"

"Oddly enough, sir," replied Sir Anthony
with sudden heat, "there is. And I want
to tell you, here and now, that you are to
desist from inflicting the same upon this dear
lady."

Cradock flashed a startled glance in the
direction of his wife.

"I don't quite follow," he said.

"Mrs. Cradock," explained Sir Anthony, "has
been honouring me with her confidence—to
this extent, that you have acquired some hold
over her, and are trading upon it. I have not
pressed Mrs. Cradock for further details——"

"Ah!" There was genuine relief in Captain
Conway's voice.

"But I should like to give you a piece of
professional information; and that is, that the
law has an ugly name for persons like you, and
an uncomfortable remedy for——"

Cradock was quite at his ease again.

"But you must first catch your hare, my

dear Sir Anthony. To employ an expression which I picked up in the United States of America, you have nothing on me."

" For the moment I admit that I have nothing on you—— "

" So that's that ! " Cradock turned away lightly, as if to address Mildred.

" But I may add that I once numbered among my acquaintances an American attaché at the Embassy in Rome, from whose vocabulary I culled many priceless flowers of American idiom."

" Such as : ' One of these days I shall catch you with the goods ! ' "

" Very apt ! Capital ! "

Uncle Tony suddenly extended an appealing hand.

" Captain Conway," he said earnestly, " you are a man of very exceptional talents and ability. Why don't you run straight ? Why don't you play the game ? "

Cradock laughed, pleasantly enough.

" Too boring, my old friend. Too humdrum ! Too—easy ! Life is so much more entertaining if one avoids the beaten path of virtue. That's my answer. Now I want a little chat with Mrs. Cradock. Will you excuse us ? "

" Certainly—not ! " said Uncle Tony, sitting heavily upon a chair.

Cradock made an almost imperceptible signal to his wife. She stepped forward mechanically.

"Please, Uncle Tony!" she said.

Uncle Tony reluctantly uprooted himself.

"Very well, my dear," he said. "But, in leaving this gentleman on your premises, may I recommend you—again quoting my friend the attaché—to have all your furniture screwed to the floor? *Au revoir*, Captain Conway—until Philippi!"

"Do you know," said Cradock pleasantly, "I believe that old man was trying to be rude to me?"

"What do you want this time?" asked Mildred, in an utterly expressionless voice.

"Well, I am killing two birds with one stone. I am deputising for Denny—who is down at my bungalow entertaining a few of my friends and asks to be excused from taking you on the river—and I want to talk business with you."

"And I want to talk business with you!" replied Mildred, in sudden anger. "I'm not going to have my friends robbed. You must pay back those cheques and postal orders that you stole this afternoon."

Denis Cradock made himself comfortable upon the sofa.

"My dear Milly," he said, "fair exchange is no robbery. If there was any unfairness, it was to myself. I collected eighty-seven pounds odd, and I am giving a perfectly good cheque for one hundred pounds in return—or rather, you are, which makes the transaction even

more impeccable." He laughed. " Now, my
dear, I'm all attention. What's your trouble ? "

Mildred took her stand before him resolutely.

" This sort of thing can't go on," she said ;
" it's too shameful. You've made me stand
sponsor for you ; you've robbed my friends—— "

" Only of very trifling sums, as yet."

" That makes it more shameful. They were
such mean little thefts."

" But you must be reasonable, Milly.
Remember, most of the people here are in very
moderate circumstances. If they had more
money, I would take it."

But Mildred was in no mood for persiflage.

" You've pilfered," she continued ; " you've
cheated ; you've sponged on every one. You've
borrowed money which you don't mean to pay
back ; you've made love to foolish women like
Laura Meakin—— "

Cradock interrupted her again.

" In justice to myself, my dear, I must tell
you that there are others who do more credit
to my taste than dear Laura. There's a perfect
little darling at the dairy farm, beyond—— "

" I think we may take your list of conquests
as read. I've known you for a good many years
now," Mildred reminded him. " Well, to cut
a long story short, you're living the life of a
parasite—partly on me, which I can stand ;

partly on my friends, which I can't. But all that is a trifle, compared with the rest."

" The rest ? "

" Yes—the human part. You've been trying to separate my children from me."

" Dear, dear, have I ? "

" Yes, ever since you arrived. You've made little headway with Joan—— "

Cradock grinned ruefully.

" You're right there. I got no change out of Joan. They're strange, hard creatures, modern daughters."

" But "—Mildred's eyes blazed—" you're demoralising Denny. I believe you're leading him into bad ways. He's not so frank with me as he used to be. He talked a lot of quite new nonsense to me the other day—about apron-strings, and the necessity of a man living his own life and sowing his own wild oats, and all the pernicious rigmarole with which creatures like you try to stimulate immature boys into making a mess of their lives before they have had a chance to find themselves. That's what you've been doing ! "

Cradock nodded.

" In other words," he said, " I have been keeping my end up." He rose lazily, and strolled to the sideboard, in search of sherry. " My dear Milly, you know my philosophy of

I

life—my *Credo*. I believe in Number One. I
believe that the fools and the rich were sent
into the world for the wise and the poor to
live on. I believe in brains. I believe in
grasping opportunities as they arise. I believe
in fighting with such weapons as fortune puts
into my hand. The best of all weapons is a
hostage. Fortune has given me two—my son
and my daughter. Can you blame me if I
employ them against you ? It's war between
us, isn't it ? "

" To the knife ! " The words came from
between Mildred's closed teeth.

" Then why," inquired Cradock blandly,
" criticise me for trying to win ? You must
be consistent, you know."

But Mildred was consistent enough upon one
point.

" You're demoralising Denny," she repeated
doggedly, " and I'm going to stop it."

" How do you propose to set about it, my
dear ? "

Mildred's answer surprised him. She came
closer, and looked up earnestly, almost eagerly,
into his face.

" How much will you take to go right away
from here ? " she asked.

" Where on earth to ? "

" New York—Cape Town—anywhere ! I would

pay you an allowance—a big allowance. You could apply for it personally every month." She was speaking a little breathlessly. " Denis, I would give you a lot ! I could live on very little ; and—and once I got the children settled in life, I would send it all—every penny of it. Denis—please ! "

Her answer was an enigmatical smile—half mockery, half genuine admiration.

" You look amazingly attractive when you plead, Milly—*and* young ! But I have an alternative to propose."

" Yes, yes ? " She was willing to snatch at any straw.

" Of course it's a modest proposal, because I can't afford to push you too hard. If I do, your abnormal maternal instincts will drive you out into the open, and the whole story will become public property. Result, disaster —domestic and social for you, universal and absolute for me ! I suppose, if we do get down to bare knuckles, you'll employ the law to fling me out of this house altogether ? "

" Yes. I lie awake at night now, wondering whether it wouldn't be wiser to do it, once and for all."

" Precisely. But first of all, this offer of yours. Is it quite kind, quite Christian ? What is it that you're asking me to do—me ?

—your husband, and the father of your children? To separate myself for ever from my attractive wife and my attractive son and daughter, and to retire to some remote foreign seaport, to live the life of—what? A remittance man!"

"Aren't you a remittance man now?"

"Oh dear, no. A remittance man is paid to stay abroad and drink himself to death; you are paying me to stay here and keep sober."

Mildred broke away from him impatiently.

"For heaven's sake, don't be facetious now!" she said. "What's your alternative?"

"This. As you are doubtless aware"— Cradock turned away and surveyed himself complacently in the adjacent mirror—" I have made quite a hit in this neighbourhood, as an eligible *parti*. Young persons with shingled hair languish after me. Laura Meakin has as good as laid her heart and gilt-edged securities at my feet. Several more of your friends are consumed by a hopeless passion for me." He turned to his wife again. " And do you know why they regard that passion as hopeless? Because they have made up their minds, collectively, that you are the lucky one!"

" *Oh!* " Mildred clenched her fists frantically. The man was incorrigible.

" Yes. Milly, in our declining years you and

I find ourselves the central figures of a romance —a romance manufactured for us by these worthy, sentimental, chuckle-headed neighbours of yours. Isn't that wonderful? My suggestion is that we do not disappoint them. In other words, let Mildred Cradock take Dale Conway for her second husband, and put the parish out of its misery!" He laid down his glass, took Mildred by the shoulders, gently enough, and turned her towards him. "Mrs. Cradock, will you marry me?"

Mildred met his gaze steadily.

"Never in the world, my friend!" she said.

Having failed to carry matters by assault, Denis Cradock sat down, composedly enough, and proceeded to invest the position.

"Imagine the advantages of such an arrangement," he said.

"They certainly call for some imagination!"

"We all stand to profit by it. You would profit——"

"I? Good heavens!"

"Yes; it would be a great economy for you. It must be very expensive, having to board me out and run me as a separate show."

"It is cheap at the price," replied Mildred simply.

"The children would profit," continued

Cradock. " You object to acknowledge me as their father, because you say it would demoralise them to know that my undesirable blood runs in their veins. Very well. But if I become their stepfather, that objection is overruled, isn't it ? Besides "—he smiled impudently— " think how useful you would find me."

" Useful ? "

" Yes, as an object lesson. When I was good, you could point me out as a shining example ; when, if ever, I was bad, you could employ me as an awful warning."

Mildred shivered, not altogether from a sense of repulsion. The rogue's amazing magnetism was beginning to make itself felt : the old fascination was coming back.

" Please don't be ridiculous," she said.

" And lastly," pursued Cradock, " there is my own little point of view. I should profit too : I admit it frankly. I should be restored to my position—my rightful position, Mildred ! —of husband and father. My children would not know that I was theirs, but I at least would know that they were mine." There was the faintest suspicion of a quiver in his voice now. Mildred was quite familiar with that quiver. She stiffened again promptly.

" Is that all ? " she asked. " Because if it is, I think you'd better go now."

Her husband rose suddenly from his chair, and came across the room to her.

" No, it isn't all," he said. " Milly "—again came the little quiver—" when you married me you loved me, didn't you ? "

" Need we go into that ? " she asked stonily.

" And you love me still, Milly ! " He broke off, and gazed down upon her, holding his breath. He was fighting with his back to the wall now, and both knew it. She looked up into his face steadily.

" Twenty years ago," she said, " I thought there was no man in the world like you. Now I merely hope so ! "

He came a step nearer. " That's not a very direct answer, Milly. Anyhow, you loved me once, and I loved you—and I do still ! " He turned on his heel and walked slowly towards the open window. " That's all. I just wanted you to know."

" Don't lie to me, Denis," she said faintly.

He whirled round. " It isn't a lie. It's the truth—the truth ! And you know it ! "

Mildred shook her head.

" No, it's not. You think it is : I'll give you credit for that. You've a real gift for creating a convincing atmosphere, as many a woman has discovered to her cost ; and you tell a tale with such real dramatic instinct that

you sometimes end by believing it yourself.
You thought you were being quite sincere just
now."

" I was! I am!"

But Mildred shook her head again—sorrowfully, almost tenderly.

" No. I have known you for twenty-two
years, you see, and it won't do. If I thought
there was any truth in that last statement of
yours—one single live spark of truth or sincerity
—I might find it in my heart to forgive you
everything, and give you another chance. But
there isn't. You're only acting, Denis. You
don't think you're acting, but you are. What
you said just now was simply an inspiration
of the moment. You'll realise that in five
minutes."

She turned away from him, and walked
slowly through the open door to the foot of the
staircase. But she had not yet pierced Denis
Cradock's armour—the impenetrable armour of
the self-hypnotised. He followed her into the
hall.

" It was the truth, Milly," he said doggedly.

" Believe me, I know better."

" It was the truth! I came here purposely
to tell it to you. Listen! You say I am a
bad egg. Perhaps I am. You say I live by
my wits, on my friends. Perhaps I do. You

say I have treated you badly. I certainly have. You say I would demoralise my own children. Perhaps I should. You say I am every kind of heartless, cold-blooded, deliberate schemer. Well, I am a lot of things, but I'm not that. I'm human, and I love you, and I believe you love me! Milly, give me a sporting chance! Trust me this once! Take me back! I swear I'll be a good husband to you. If ever I fail you again I promise faithfully to walk straight out of this house and out of your life for good and all. Milly, don't look away—look at me! Look into my face with the old look! Milly!"

He took her hands and drew her towards him. She began to shake. She was weakening, and she felt somehow glad. Despite herself, her heart rose. Out in the garden someone was whistling cheerfully. But she would not yield yet.

"Denis," she said, "I—I don't know. You're so volatile, so impulsive! If only I could be sure!"

Her husband did not reply. He was gazing into her eyes, eagerly, feverishly, like a lover of twenty.

"It's coming back!" he cried exultantly. "The look—the old look—it's coming back! Milly!"

"Denis!"

r*

She swayed towards him; then suddenly paused, and stepped back. The whistling outside had ceased, for the whistler had entered the room behind them, and now stood framed in the doorway leading into the hall. It was Master Denny Cradock, a little flushed of face and bright of eye.

"Hallo, Conway, old son!" he cried hilariously. "Your cocktails are the absolute goods—and that little fair girl is a peach! It'll be a wonderful trip. They're all outside in the punt now, with Bags. Shall I bring them in? Carried unanimously! Hallo, Mum! I didn't see you!"

"Denny," said Mildred, quickly, "I want to speak to you. Don't go away." The tone of her voice brought her mildly exhilarated offspring to his senses at once.

"All right, Mum. I'll tell them to trickle away."

He disappeared, shouting a movement order to the party in the punt, and leaving an uncanny silence behind him. His parents returned heavily into the morning-room.

"So you were lying again?" said Mildred.

Cradock shrugged his shoulders, and smiled ruefully.

"I suppose I was," he said; "but, honestly, I didn't know I was. You swept me off my feet, Milly : I was up in the clouds." He pointed an accusing finger. " And so were you ! "

" Well, we have come down to earth," she replied composedly—" for good." Then she blazed out. " What is all this about a trip ? What are you plotting to do ? "

" That," replied Cradock, quite himself again, " was what is known in military circles as an alternative scheme. Having failed in one line of approach, I am now going to try another. In other words, I am reluctantly compelled to apply that screw."

" What do you mean ? " asked Mildred, in sudden fear.

" I am going to get to work on one of my hostages."

" What are you going to do to him ? "

" Nothing very dreadful. I'm going to take him away on a little pleasure excursion."

" Where ? "

" You can ask Denny. But I must point out, Milly, that when, if ever, he comes back, it will be on my terms and not yours. Here he is "—as the hostage under discussion re-entered by the window. " Come along, Denny ! Come and give me your moral support in the humble petition which I am presenting."

" Righto ! " said Denny, a little self-consciously.

"Denny," said Mildred, going straight to him, "what is this trip you were speaking of?"

Denny inserted three fingers under his collar, and swallowed.

"Well, Mother," he said, "the fact is, I've been in training for weeks and weeks—and—er —weeks——"

"And he stroked his crew to victory this afternoon," supplemented Cradock.

"And now that it's all over, I—I—was just wondering if it wouldn't be a good plan to ease up a bit—unbend the old bow, so to speak. And as Captain Conway happens to be going up to town for a few days, and has very kindly offered to take me with him, it seemed to me that it would be a sound scheme to—er— accept. After that, we thought of joining a little party of Captain Conway's friends on a trip to the Continent. Those old historical places, you know—Paris, and so forth. Denny swallowed again, and turned to his prospective host. "Aren't we, old man?"

"If Mrs. Cradock has no objection," said Conway gravely. "I was just sounding her on the subject when you came in." He turned to Mildred. "The idea is this. My old friends, the Moons——"

"Those people who come to the meeting?" There was no mistaking Mildred's alarm now.

"Mrs. Moon," announced Denny stoutly, "is an old dear. She will chaperon us."

"Chaperon? There will be other ladies, then?"

"Yes," said Cradock—"two of Mrs. Moon's nieces. Nice, unaffected girls."

"What about it, Mother?" asked Denny, putting his fate to the touch.

Mildred hesitated, as well she might. There was only one thing to be said; the difficulty was to say it without playing straight into the hands of the enemy.

"I don't want to lay down the law, Denny," she began slowly, "but—— "

It was as she feared. Denny fired up at once.

"Oh, Mother! I can't be tied to your apron strings all my life!"

"I would be personally responsible for Denny, Mrs. Cradock," said Conway.

This interposition may have been well meant, but it had an unexpected effect. Mildred suddenly lost control of herself. She threw her arms round her son's neck.

"Denny," she cried, "you're not going with that man!"

"I say, Mother! Really!" Every fibre of Denny's youthful reserve was tingling. "Don't make me look ridiculous! I'm trying hard not to lose my temper; but do think! Think what a fool I feel, being cried over because

I'm going on a holiday for a couple of weeks ! "

Mildred recovered her poise.

" I'm sorry, Denny," she said ; " but I'm in a terribly difficult position, and I can ask no one to advise me."

" You have a grown-up son," Denny pointed out stiffly.

Mildred smiled, despite herself.

" Bless you ! " she said. " But I can't ask you about this."

" May I come in ? " Uncle Tony stood in the window.

" Of course, dear Uncle Tony," said Mildred. " Do you want me for anything ? "

" No ; emphatically no ! If anybody is wanted, it is Captain Conway. I have just encountered two of your friends in the garden, Captain Conway—Mr. and Mrs. Moon."

" Are they coming in here ? " asked Conway quickly.

" Mr. Moon appears anxious to call ; Mrs. Moon less so. I understood Mr. Moon—whose speech was unfortunately obscured by a certain thickness of utterance, doubtless temporary— to say that it was his desire to come and say *au revoir* to his late hostess. Mrs. Moon banned the project, on the grounds, explicitly expressed, that when Moon had had a couple he always mucked things up. I supported

Mrs. Moon, and between us we effected a merciful eclipse of the heavenly body under discussion."

Uncle Tony discharged this little *mot* with undisguised satisfaction ; but Cradock laughed.

" Moon's a funny old fellow," he said, " and his heart's a bit dicky. He ought not to be out in this hot sun at all. I'll go and look after him presently. Has Denny disclosed to you the little conspiracy, Sir Anthony ? "

" Which of them ? "

" Well, it's this way. Denny and I have much in common. One of our joint characteristics is a shrinking from monotony. We are both, just a little—may I say ?—fed up with rural felicity. After all, a backwater is only a backwater."

" How true ! " said Uncle Tony politely.

" And since Denny and I are feeling a trifle stagnant, I have suggested a little excursion."

" Where to ? "

" London, certainly ; Paris, probably ; Deauville, possibly."

Uncle Tony turned to Denny.

" What about ways and means, Denny ? "

" Denny will be my guest," said Cradock quickly.

" Denny will not be your guest ! " It was Mildred speaking again, white with anger.

" Mother, Mother ! " cried Denny genuinely shocked.

That experienced diplomat, Sir Anthony Fenwick, realised that he was participating in a domestic crisis, and that the next move lay with him.

" May I put my oar in ? " he asked, and continued :

" Denny, I am not in your mother's confidence, but I am inclined to think she may have some substantial reason for her objection which she is not at liberty to disclose. Don't you think we might take her word for it, and endeavour to meet her wishes ? "

" To do so," replied poor, pompous Denny, " without some sort of explanation or apology, would be a direct slight to my friend Captain Conway."

Sir Anthony smiled grimly.

" Perhaps your friend stands less in need of an explanation—or an apology—than we imagine," he said.

Denny caught the implication.

" What do you mean, Uncle Tony ? What does he mean, Conway ? "

" I have no idea, Denny. But apparently my character is in question : I am not regarded as a suitable companion for innocent youth. You, Denny, are the innocent youth. Very well ; I never crowd in where I'm not wanted Good afternoon ! "

Cradock took up his hat. But Denny, crimson with anger and mortification, started forward.

" Damn it all, Conway," he cried, " you shan't be insulted like this ! Do you think I'm going to stay here any longer ? Not on your life ! I'm coming with you. And "— with a ferocious glare in the direction of his mother and uncle—" if I can't be treated decently at home, I won't come back—there ! It's no good, Mother. Please don't stand in my way ! "

But Mildred stood in his path, with arms outstretched, and a look on her face that Denny had never seen before.

" Listen ! " she said. Her voice was hard and dry, and her eyes were set. " I have something to say, and I must say it. I had hoped and prayed that I might never have to say it ; but—I see I must." She pointed towards her husband. " I'm going to tell you all about that man—— "

" Don't be a fool, Mildred ! " said Cradock hastily.

Mildred took no notice. A rattling noise was audible outside—the song of the local Ford from the station. But she did not hear it ; neither did anyone else in the room.

" My mind's made up," she said. " Denny, dear, I told you children that this man was an old friend—a brother-officer of your father's."

"Yes, Mother?" said Denny in a startled voice.

"He's nothing of the kind." Her voice rose desperately. "He's——"

From the hall outside came the crash of a slammed front door; feet were heard racing towards the morning-room. There was a flash of a white frock and two attenuated black legs, and next moment—flushed, radiant, and mysteriously sent from heaven—Molly Cradock was hanging round her mother's neck.

"Hallo, Mum, darling! I'm home! I'm home! We've got the mumps! Isn't it lovely? Hallo, Denny, dear! We've broken up! We've got the mumps!" By this time she was racing round the room, distributing promiscuous embraces. "Uncle Tony, we've got the mumps—and we're infectious! Give me a kiss!" She saluted her dazed but submissive relative upon both cheeks; then, instinctively jibbing from the unfamiliar figure by the window, flew back to Mildred. "Oh, Mum!"

Mildred clung to her.

"My dear, my dear!" she murmured. "My Littlest! Bless you for coming!" And she meant what she said, in a way which Molly never dreamed of, then or thereafter.

It was Denny who spoke next.

"I say," he exclaimed, "who is that perfectly lovely girl out in the garden?"

"Hoo!" gasped Molly in a fresh flutter of excitement, "I'd forgotten. That's Phyllis."

"Phyllis who?" asked her brother, gazing ardently out of the window.

"Phyllis Harding. She had nowhere to go, so I brought her here. She's infectious too. Come and bring her in, Denny. Come along, Uncle Tony!"

She dashed out, with Youth and Age after her, neck and neck. The vision in the garden was plainly an attractive one. Mildred and Denis Cradock were left alone.

"We can't go on with this now," Mildred said helplessly. "Come here to-morrow, and we'll try to——"

But Cradock did not appear to be listening; he was gazing out of the window after the receding figure of Molly.

"Who is she?" he asked eagerly. There was a curious unfamiliar ring in his voice. "That child—who is she?"

"She is my other daughter—and yours."

Denis Cradock gazed at his wife, fascinated.

"Mine?" he said slowly. "I never knew!"

"No. She came to me after you left me. I'm glad no one has mentioned her to you."

Cradock nodded his head.

" I see. Your favourite, evidently ? "

" Yes. And if you dare to lay one grimy finger upon her soul ; if you dare to dispel one single illusion in the little white palace of dreams that she lives in—I'll kill you with my own hands, so help me God ! "

Cradock shrank back, genuinely appalled. He had never seen his wife like this ; nor indeed had anyone else.

Suddenly cheerful voices broke the silence, and the troupe re-entered, escorting the vision from the garden. Denny had possessed himself of her bag, a receptacle measuring possibly eight inches square. Uncle Tony had retrieved an umbrella. Molly was dancing ahead.

" Mum," she announced, " this is Phyllis Harding ! She's a prefect," she added, in a hoarse and reverent whisper.

Mildred embraced her unexpected guest with her usual quiet cordiality.

" How do you do, dear ? " she said. " I'm glad Molly had the sense to bring you."

Miss Harding flushed prettily.

" Thank you so much," she said, in a low voice. " My people are in India ; so—— "

" Here is someone who will tell you all about India," announced Mildred. She indicated Sir Anthony, who seized the opportunity to shake hands for the second time

Captain Conway was next introduced, but greeted the vision with less intensity than might have been expected. His attention was focused elsewhere.

" Would you like to come out into the garden, Miss Harding ? " suggested Denny, utilising the first interval of silence. " You've just missed the Regatta, but there'll be fireworks to-night. I'll take you out in a canoe," he added hurriedly, evidently fearful lest a maturer rival should forestall him.

" Oh, thank you," said Miss Harding, turning her dark eyes upon him.

The pair passed out of the window together. On the way Denny collided with an arm-chair and tripped over the window-sill, but did not appear to notice.

" Heigho ! " said Uncle Tony sorrowfully. " Si vieillesse pouvait ! "

Another voice broke in—a voice with an odd, strained ring about it.

" Will you please introduce me to this young lady, Mrs. Cradock ? "

Mildred turned.

" I quite forgot," she said, smiling. " This is my Littlest—Molly. Molly, this is Captain Conway, a very old friend of ours."

Molly shook hands with her usual cordiality ; then looked up suddenly.

"An old friend ? " she asked. Then, with a rush :

"Did you know my father ? "

Cradock looked down upon her, still holding her small, eager hand. He smiled.

"Know your father, Molly ? None better ! "

"O—o—oh ! " Molly emitted a rapturous sigh, and shook hands again. The stranger continued to regard her curiously. Apparently the sight of Molly had aroused in him some unfamiliar emotion.

"I never heard about you, Molly," he said. He turned to Mildred, with mock severity. "Why haven't I been told about Molly ? " he asked.

"I can't think."

He pointed to the little table by the fireplace.

"Why is Molly's portrait not in the family gallery ? "

"Hallo, Mother ! " said Molly, following his gaze ; "what's happened to my photo ? "

"I took it upstairs, dear."

"And I know why," said Cradock. "You were jealous ! Tell me, Molly, aren't you your mother's favourite ? "

"Oh, no ! " replied Molly seriously. "Mother has no favourites ; you ask her."

"I know she has ! You're the favourite ; and she didn't want to share even your name with—an outsider like me."

" I'm sure you're not an outsider ! "

" There, you see ? " exclaimed Cradock triumphantly. " I have a supporter in this household at last ! " He took up his hat again. " It's settled, then, that I come to lunch to-morrow ? Thank you ? *Au revoir* ! "

" I'll show you the gate," said Molly, all solicitude. She reached up and slipped her arm into his. " This way—out of the window and across the lawn."

The pair strode silently to the window. Then Molly broke in again.

" I ought to warn you," she said ; " I'm infectious. I may give you something."

Cradock looked down upon her, and smiled.

" I don't think you can give me anything, Molly, that I haven't had already."

The pair disappeared, and their voices died away. Uncle Tony turned to Mildred.

" I'm not so sure," he said ; " I'm not so sure ! "

"So that's the real story?" said Uncle Tony.

He was sitting under the beech tree on the lawn after dinner, hardly visible except for the glow of his cigar. Mildred, a dim vision in white, reclined in a deep cane chair beside him. The river was audible close by, rippling against the roots of the willows. A boat carrying a gramophone was drifting past on the far side, the raucosity of the accursed instrument mellowed by transmission over water. A mile upstream, over Ripleigh Reach, the sky was intermittently illuminated by fireworks and set pieces. Excited shouts came floating down the soft night breeze.

"Yes," said Mildred, "you know it all now." She extended a tired hand, and laid it on her uncle's. "Having told you, old friend, I feel that I can go on again. I very nearly gave up this afternoon: if Molly hadn't dropped in on us from the skies I should have shrieked out the whole story. I feel stronger now—since I've confessed."

"A trouble shared is a trouble halved. Hallo, what's that?"

There was a crash and a shriek in mid-stream,

and the gramophone ceased to function. Sounds of an altercation followed, during which one gentleman was heard recommending another gentleman to fry his face.

" What's the matter ? " asked Mildred, as Sir Anthony rose and peered across the river.

" Nothing serious. Ships that can't pass in the night, that's all."

" Steering isn't too easy. The river is running strongly after this week's downpour."

" So I noticed this afternoon, as I watched Master Leo Bagby contending with his punt-pole. It was lucky for the crews they hadn't to row up-stream, or our young light-weights would have had a bad time of it." The old gentleman sat down again. " Now—what are we going to do about it ? "

" What do you advise, Uncle Tony ? "

" My advice to you is the advice which I have been offering to people throughout the forty years of my extremely undiplomatic career. When in doubt, tell the truth ! Tell your children who this man is."

" That would involve telling them what he is, and—what their mother is. Uncle Tony, I couldn't ! The shame of it, for them ! A father like that, and a liar for a mother—a liar for all these years ! I couldn't ! I couldn't ! "

" I don't think," said Uncle Tony soberly, " that you need fear your children's verdict on that particular count, Mildred."

"Still, I can't do it. I realised that the moment Molly burst in on us this afternoon. They mustn't know about the—about the—the—— "

" The stock they sprang from—eh ? I see your point." Uncle Tony turned thoughtfully to his niece. " Mildred, what is this man's price ? I am sure he has one."

Mildred shook her head.

" I've offered him all the money I have, to go away ; but he won't."

" Why should he ? He knows a soft berth when he sees one. Our job is to make him realise how precarious his position is. If his identity is revealed, he will *have* to go—to gaol, for all we know. Hasn't he any proposal to make—any compromise to offer ? "

" Yes. That was what he came about this afternoon. He wants me to take him as my second husband."

Sir Anthony was fairly startled this time.

" To marry him—again ? "

" Yes. Go through the ceremony as if it were something quite new to us both."

" H'm ! It's an ingenious suggestion. I can see his point of view : your lips permanently sealed, and free board and lodging for life for him. Incidentally, he would find himself in the unique position of second husband to a wife who couldn't possibly cast up to him the

virtues of her first! He's a humorous rogue,
Still, I don't quite see where you come in."

"No. I don't suppose he thought of that."

"I'm quite certain he didn't. You refused,
of course?"

"Of course. It would be a living lie—and
I've lied enough."

"What then? You said this afternoon you
thought there was an alternative."

"Yes," said Mildred in a low voice. "I—
I could go back to him."

"Back to him?"

"Yes—by myself. Not immediately, of
course," she explained hurriedly; "but in a
few years' time. I'll promise him that—with
every penny I have thrown in—if only he'll go
right away and not come back until I have had
a chance to get the children settled in life.
After all, they're getting pretty big now—
aren't they? Joan is as good as engaged to
Leo, so she's no anxiety. Denny will soon be
able to keep himself. Molly "—her voice shook
here—" Molly will soon grow up, and—and—
marry some nice boy. I shall be quite an
independent lady then, able to give my whole
time to—my husband. I think he needs me,
Uncle Tony. I think it's what I ought to have
decided on all along."

Uncle Tony rose to his feet.

" My God, Mildred," he said, " you're a brave woman ! "

" No, I'm not. I'm a fearful coward, really ; but I happen to be a mother, I suppose."

" Well, I don't happen to be a mother, but I know courage when I meet it."

Mildred sighed.

" It's terribly hard, being courageous, Uncle Tony. I suppose to a man it comes natural ; but——"

" Man ? Don't you believe it ! The average man is the most pusillanimous creature alive —the average woman has seven times his pluck."

Mildred shook her head.

"It's sweet of you to try to cheer me up," she said, " but I can't believe that. Look at the things our men did in the war."

" Yes ; and I bet most of them were in a blue funk while they were doing them. In my young days I had to do them myself, and I know." Sir Anthony sat down again. " Has it ever occurred to you, Mildred, to consider why men do brave things—or, for that matter, honourable things ? "

" Because they are brave and honourable men, I suppose."

" Stuff and nonsense ! Most of us are arrant cowards or natural rapscallions. Such efforts as we make in the direction of courage or virtue are prompted as often as not by a childish desire to live up to a standard set for us by someone else. That's what it comes to. Believe me, Mildred, many a man has won the Victoria Cross with his heart in his boots, simply because some fuzzy-headed little nonentity in a jazz jumper at Tooting has taken it for granted from the start that he was going to win it, and he didn't dare go home without it. It's the same with our morals. We keep straight—we do the big thing—not because we're naturally virtuous or generous, but from a foolish pride in living up to some still more foolish person's estimate of us."

Mildred rose to her feet.

"Dear Uncle Tony," she said softly, "I believe you're talking all this nonsense just to get me back out of my black mood."

"Nonsense!" exclaimed Sir Anthony indignantly. "It's golden truth! I give women up!" He took her hand in his, to prove his words. "And you would renounce everything —your pleasant position, and your pleasant neighbours—to go back to that fellow?"

"Yes, if it would help."

"Does he want you?"

"He says so."

"Do you think he loves you?"

"I don't see how he can. I know too much about his character. A man can forgive a woman anything but that. But he seems to need me."

" May I ask one more impertinent question ?
Do you—love him ? "

Mildred's grip tightened.

" When I married him," she replied steadily,
" I gave him everything. And I'm not the
sort that asks for things back again."

Uncle Tony gently released her hand, and
nodded.

" I understand," he said—" so far as a man
can. Is that someone talking ? "

" Yes. It sounds like Denny and Miss
Harding. The backwater runs up this way,
just beyond those laurels. I think they're
getting a boat out."

Denny's voice broke clear, close by—Denny's
voice of ceremony.

" Take my hand, Miss Harding; it's pretty murky
here." There came a rustling sound, as of chiffon
brushing against foliage. " That's right; here we are!
Now, shall we have the canoe, or the electric punt?
The punt is the safest; the canoe the snuggest."

" Let's have the canoe," replied the demure
voice of Miss Phyllis Harding.

Considerable commotion followed—the commotion of extreme solicitude.

" Here we are ! " said Denny at last. " Here's
a cushion for your back, and here's a paddle
for you. You needn't use it if you don't want to.
I'll do the donkey work."

Miss Harding spoke again.

" I think it's wonderful, all you know about boats, Mr. Cradock," she said.

" I should be a pretty fair rotter if I didn't. I've spent all my life on the river, you know."

" I see. Were you rowing in the Regatta to-day ? "

" Oh, in a small way."

" I like him for saying that," murmured Sir Anthony.

" Now for a cigarette," continued Denny, " and we'll push off. I think you said you didn't smoke ? "

" No. I'm afraid it's stupid of me."

" I think it shows great character."

" Oh, do you, Mr. Cradock ? " Miss Harding was plainly gratified—and surprised.

" Yes," said Denny firmly. " Half the girls I know only smoke because they're afraid to refuse. It's the same with cocktails, and things like that."

" I don't like them, either."

" I'm delighted to hear it. I hate to see women drinking."

" Then "—Miss Harding's voice sounded more demure than ever—" you don't think me old-fashioned ? "

" Old fashions," announced Denny with intense solemnity, " are the best."

" Is Saul also among the prophets ? " inquired Sir Anthony of his niece.

" The fact is," continued Denny, with all the zeal of the recently reformed, " you get to know the modern girl so quickly that, before you know where you are, you know her too well—and *there* you are ! Why, Miss Harding, some of them get quite ratty if you don't call them by their Christian names right off."

" Oh, Mr. Cradock ! " replied Miss Harding in a shocked voice.

" Now," continued Denny, warming to his work, " I simply can't express to you what a treat it has been to meet you. It is seldom in these days that one encounters a girl with so much—er—*laissez-faire*. You are so beautifully natural—so content to be yourself, and so on. You are so—stop me if I'm annoying you."

" It's all right," said Miss Harding cordially.

" The trouble with the average girl," continued Denny, reassured, " is that she is deadly afraid of being thought simple, and—er—normal. She has to go about all the time pretending to be dissipated and *blasée*, when she isn't a bit, really."

" You're terribly critical of us, Mr. Cradock."

" Oh, I'm not criticising one sex alone. Men are just as idiotic. Miss Harding "—Denny's voice dropped to a very creditable imitation of Uncle Tony's most pontifical rumble—

" there are far more good people walking this earth pretending to be bad than bad people pretending to be good. There's nothing makes a wolf—a sheep—feel so safe as making a noise like a sheep—a wolf! Scratch a devil—— "

There came a faint squeak from Miss Harding, accompanied by strangled sounds from beneath the beech-tree, as of an Elder Statesman fighting for breath.

" Anyhow," concluded Denny, floundering to safe ground, " I think you're the most exceptional girl I've ever known in my life."

" Oh, do you ? "

" Yes."

" *Oh !* " A gentle sigh followed ; then prolonged silence.

" We appear to be eavesdropping," murmured Uncle Tony. " Perhaps it would be kind to do something about it." He rose, and coughed raucously. " I'm going into the house for another cigar," he proclaimed.

" All right, Uncle Tony," cried Mildred. " I'll wait here for you."

Sir Anthony shaped a cautious course through the soft darkness, and presently arrived upon the little landing-stage which projected into the tree-girt backwater. Here a certain amount of illumination was provided by a row of Chinese lanterns on a string. He found two extremely

k

self-conscious young people, reclining at opposite
ends of a Canadian canoe.

"Hallo, Denny!" he said. "Enjoying the
fireworks?"

"Rather, Uncle Tony!" replied Denny, with
great heartiness.

"You don't get a very good view from here."

"No, you don't. The fact is, we're a bit
late in starting. Miss Harding, we must bustle
about. What about it?" Denny hurriedly
unmoored the canoe. Uncle Tony, having
had his little joke, departed contentedly across
the lawn; but Mildred appeared in his place.

"Take care of yourselves, children," she said.

"We shall be all right, Mother," replied
Denny.

"I feel so safe, Mrs. Cradock," remarked
Phyllis, "with Mr. Cradock."

Mildred smiled, and was upon the point of
following Uncle Tony, when Denny, with a
hurried apology to his passenger, scrambled out
of the canoe and followed her.

"Mother," he said, in a low voice, "I'm
sorry I was rude to you this afternoon. I lost
my temper."

"That's all right, dear," said Mildred, with
a sudden access of happiness. She placed her
hands upon her tall son's shoulders, and reached
up to kiss him. Denny responded readily

enough ; then stood hesitating, as if trying to bring himself to say something further. Finally, he turned away.

" Now then, Miss Harding," he said, " full speed ahead ! "

Grasping a gunwale in each hand, he took a running push. Next moment the canoe was gliding riverward, with an extremely silent passenger seated at either end.

Mildred watched them out of sight ; then turned to find Sir Anthony standing beside her.

" I'm glad he did that," remarked the old man.

" So am I. You saw then ? "

" Yes. Does it mean that the expedition to Paris is definitely relinquished ? "

" I'm afraid not. It was on the tip of his tongue to give it all up just now, but he couldn't quite bring himself to speak."

" Perhaps Miss Phyllis will help him to decide."

Mildred smiled. " I shouldn't wonder ! "

" It seems to be developing into a severe case," observed Sir Anthony. " She's infectious, all right ! "

" She's a very nice girl," said Mildred ; " and what's more, she's tall and dark. He's always liked them fair and fluffy before."

" That's the most cheering piece of intelligence I've heard to-day. My godson inoculated against fluff—it's almost too much to hope !

Hallo, here come the other two creatures ; I wonder what their symptoms are."

Joan and Leo appeared from the direction of the towpath and Ripleigh Reach.

" Hallo, Mother ! " cried Joan : " we've been hunting for you. We've got a seat for you in the enclosure."

" The set pieces are just coming on, sir," announced Leo to Sir Anthony. " I'll tell you how they work."

" I was afraid you would," replied Uncle Tony resignedly.

" Where's my Littlest ? " asked Mildred suddenly.

" Your leprous child ? " said Joan. " She was with us until about half an hour ago, making a public nuisance of herself on the towpath—pestering young men in blue blazers for their autographs, and probably giving them mumps in return ! "

Mildred smiled indulgently.

" She ought really to be isolated," she said. " I must go and find her."

" She's all right, Mrs. Cradock," announced Leo reassuringly. " She's on the water at present ; so the risk is limited to one gentleman."

" And who is the poor gentleman ? " asked Mildred.

" Captain Conway."

" Captain Conway ? "

" Yes." Leo was brimming over with information, as usual. " I saw them push off together from the Committee landing-stage in his punt."

" Oh ! " said Mildred, in dismay. Joan turned to her.

" They'll be all right, Mother," she said quickly.

" But I don't think she ought to be on the river at all, at this time of night—with anybody ! " said Mildred, with agitation in every note of her voice. " Please run and look for her, Leo, and tell her to come at once. Take a boat or something—anything ! "

" Righto, Mrs. Cradock."

" You go too, Joan ; you'll pick her out sooner."

" All right, Mother ! " said Joan ; and the pair ran off together.

Mildred took Sir Anthony's arm. She was trembling violently, and he helped her to a seat—a rustic bench on the little landing-stage. There she sat—shaking, despairing, almost beaten —with her dull gaze fixed on the glimmering surface of the backwater.

" It's happened," she whispered—" what I dreaded most of all ! Molly ! "

" They were bound to come together sooner or later, dear."

" But not like this—when he's in this mood !

He knows his position is desperate. He'll do anything—anything—to enlist her on his side. I know him ; I know the sort of story he'll tell her ! And she's so innocent—so credulous— so impulsive ! " Mildred flung a frightened glance out towards the dark waters of the river. " She's at his mercy out there ! She's at his mercy ! We're all at his mercy ! Uncle Tony he'll take her away from me ! "

" No he won't. No one can ever take her away from you."

" Yes, he will ! It's no use going on any longer ; I'm beaten. There's no way out." Mildred buried her face in her hands, and broke into hysterical sobbing. Her iron self-control had gone at last.

Uncle Tony took his niece's hand, and spoke in quite a new voice—the steady, even tones of a thoughtful man who is weighing his words, and who believes implicitly in what he is saying.

" Yet a little while ! " he said. " You've been so splendid so far. Listen to me, and to my confession of faith. I have been young, and now I am old ; I have had my share of the perplexities and sorrows of this world ; and they have taught me just two lessons. The first is that where human nature is concerned you never can foretell anything. A clever man is never infallibly clever ; a bad man is never utterly vile. There is a white spot on the blackest of us, and one never knows when it will not be revealed. That is one lesson ; the other is this : there is always a way out of every difficulty."

" Not always."

" Yes—always. You and I may not be able to see it, but it is there. If that had not been so the human family would not have survived for so many centuries. So long as God's writ runs on earth there will always be a way out, even though sometimes a miracle may be required to reveal it to us. We are only gropers—sometimes merely because our eyes are shut—but the light is there all the time. Courage ! "

Mildred looked up. Her face was wet—at last.

" Bless you, dear ! " she said softly. She rose, and took the old man's arm. " Shall we go into the house—and wait ? "

*   *   *   *   *

They passed slowly through the laurels, across the lawn, and out of sight.

A moment later, a long, narrow racing-punt, skilfully propelled, turned into the backwater from the river outside, and came gliding up to the little landing-stage. It contained a tall man in a dinner-jacket, and a little girl in a short pink frock. They were Denis Cradock and his daughter Molly.

"THERE!" said Cradock, bringing the punt alongside, with a dexterous flick of his paddle. "How's that for an ancient mariner?"

That small but determined hero-worshipper, Molly Cradock, buttressed about with many cushions at the other end of the punt, gave a little wriggle of pure ecstasy.

"Splendid!" she said. "I'm so sorry our voyage is over. Shall we go into the house, or will you sit here and tell me some more?"

"I don't think we'll go into the house," said Cradock. "I'm coming to lunch to-morrow, remember, and I never was one to overwork a welcome."

"I'm sure you couldn't ever do that," said Molly. "Will you come and sit beside me?" She made room for him deferentially.

"Thank you," replied Cradock. "I can just squeeze in, I think. There! Hallo, I'm sitting on something."

"It's my autograph book," said Molly, retrieving the ubiquitous volume. "I was going to ask you to write your name in it. Will you, some time ? "

" Rather ! Any old time."

Molly wriggled again. In the space of a few hours this fascinating stranger had taken complete possession of her heart ; and she realised with rapture, in some instinctive fashion of her own, that she in her turn exercised some kind of humble sway over him. Else, why should he now be reclining here, with his arm linked in hers, in a punt in a backwater obviously well content to be where he was when he might have been the centre of a gay group at the fireworks ?

The hero lit a cigar.

" This," he announced, turning his gaze towards the stars, " is bliss ! " Then he looked down upon the adoring face of his companion, pinkly illuminated by the swinging lanterns.

" Molly," he said, " do you know what you are ? "

" No. Do tell me ! "

" An oasis."

Molly's brow puckered.

" That's something shady, in a desert, isn't it ? "

Cradock smiled, perseveringly.

" Shady is a rather misleading term, Molly— especially applied to you. The shade you cast is a healing shade, always. You're a human

K*

oasis—something very rare, and soothing—— "

" O-o-oh ! " breathed Molly.

" —And refreshing—that a traveller, if he is lucky, may encounter just once or twice in his journey through—the wilderness."

" Has your journey taken you through the wilderness much ? " inquired Molly, deeply intrigued.

The wanderer shrugged his shoulders philosophically.

" I suppose it has, most of the time. I'm not kicking ; one takes the rough with the smooth. It's chiefly a matter of luck and how one begins."

" Of course it doesn't do to begin wrong," agreed Molly, nodding a wise head.

" No. But sometimes, early in life, before we are able to see very clearly ahead—when we are young, and impulsive—— "

" I'm terribly impulsive, Mother says."

" We take a step which carries us off the green path, and points us straight for the wilderness. And before we know where we are we find ourselves right in the middle of it. And some of us never get back."

" Has that happened to you ? " asked Molly, in grave concern.

" I'm afraid so, Molly."

" I'm dreadfully sorry."

" Thank you ! " There was silence again.
Plainly Molly was thinking ; and who knows
what fantastic lion-and-mouse schemes tumbled
in review through that eager little brain ?
Presently she asked :

" Are you sure you can't get back ? I mean,
couldn't you get someone to help you ? "

Cradock sighed.

" Who could ? " he said. " Who would ? "

Molly made the inevitable suggestion.

" Why not talk to Mother about it ? She's
wonderful at helping people." She waited, a
little apprehensively. Had she been too forward ? No, all was well ; he was smiling again.

" Your mother knows all about it already,
Molly," he said.

Molly's face cleared.

" Oh, I forgot ! You're old friends, aren't
you ? Of course, Mother has given you all the
help she can already "

" Yes—I suppose she has."

Molly edged a little closer.

" Captain Conway," she said shyly, " would
anybody fresh be any use ? " Then with a
rush—" Would *I* be any use ? You said something just now about stepping suddenly off the
path—into the wilderness—at the beginning.
Would you mind telling me ? I mean, how did
it happen ? "

" I married."

Molly, of course, was prepared for this.

" The wrong woman ! " she remarked, in a
hollow voice.

" Yes. No, no, Molly ; what am I saying ?
That's not fair. Perhaps I ought to say she
married the wrong man."

" How noble you are ! " remarked Molly,
with absolute sincerity. " But didn't she—
love you ? "

" I never knew. I was very, very fond
of her ; but somehow, I could never get much
response out of her. Perhaps it was my fault
Perhaps I was too rough a diamond for her."
He was speaking in a low voice, with a hand over
his eyes.

" I'm quite sure it wasn't that," said Molly
stoutly.

Cradock looked up again and smiled.

" You're a great little partisan ! "

Molly, much gratified, inquired respectfully :

" Would it hurt you to tell me the rest ? "

" There's not much to tell. She left me
at last. Perhaps she was justified : she couldn't
help being a little ashamed of me, I suppose.
She was my superior in station and she had a
good deal of money."

" She sounds mean to me."

" We mustn't judge her too hardly ; we all

have our weaknesses. God knows I have my share ! "

" Is she still alive ? "

" Yes."

" I bet she's sorry now ! "

" It's not impossible."

" People get wiser as they get older."

" How do you know, Molly ? "

" It stands to reason I'm wiser to-day than I was two years ago, I hope. You wouldn't believe the silly things I used to say and think. I thought the Derby was run *at* Derby—instead of Ascot ! I expect she's sorry all right. Is she alone ? "

" She has the children."

" Oh ! " There was infinite tragedy in Molly's voice now. " So it cut you off from your children, too ? Is she in England ? "

" Yes."

There was a very long pause. Molly was sitting up with her arms clasped round her knees, which were under her chin, gazing vacantly into that mysterious region where she spent so much of her time and from which, as her mother knew, she had never entirely emerged. The man beside her sat motionless, expressionless—waiting.

At last Molly stirred.

" Well, what's the big thought ? " he asked.

" I was thinking," replied Molly, with the air of a General who has at last hit upon the key to an impregnable position, " that I would like better than anything else in this world to find out where your wife is, and get to know her really well, and, when I had found out if she was truly sorry—and I am sure she is— I would tell her where to find you. That's what I would like to do."

Cradock's mouth twitched.

" You aren't at all impulsive, are you ? " he said.

Molly drew back quickly.

" You're laughing at me ! "

" On the contrary ! "

" I get it from my father—being impulsive, I mean. Mother has often told me about the impulsive things he used to do—suddenly give someone all the money he had in his pocket, and things like that—just because he felt sorry for them."

Cradock recalled the incident now—a characteristic act of unnecessary generosity on his part towards the shivering beggar one winter night in Cape Town. He had forgotten all about it, but Mildred had remembered.

" Your mother told you that ? "

" Yes. But of course I needn't tell you all these things. You knew him ! I envy you for that."

" Why, Molly ? "

" Because I never saw him and he never saw me. I was born after he died."

Cradock nodded his head thoughtfully.

" I must say," he said, " the revelation of your existence rather took me by surprise this afternoon. I hadn't bargained for you, Molly, somehow."

" Bargained for me ? "

" No. I thought I knew everything there was to be known about Denis Cradock—and all the time I never knew he had another daughter ! "

" Still," persisted Molly, " you *knew* him ! "

" As I know myself."

" Were you brother-officers ? "

" Yes."

" You were on the *Gallia* when she went down ? "

" Yes."

" Did you see the way he died ? "

Cradock glanced down sharply, but there was no *arrière pensée* in this proud, eager question.

" No," he said. " I was in another part of the ship."

" Of course. You would be looking after your men, like him."

" Yes, naturally."

Molly's voice softened.

" You know how he died, I suppose ? "

" I never heard the full story."

" Mother told it to me as soon as I was big enough to understand, and I've heard it from her so often since that I almost feel now as if I had been there and seen everything."

" Will you tell me the story, Molly ? "

" All right, but I've got it so much by heart that I'll have to tell it to you in Mother's words, not mine. And some of it may sound rather childish ; I was *very* little, when first—— "

" I'll understand. Go ahead, Molly ! "

Molly rose to a kneeling position, with her hands in her lap.

" Once upon a time," she began, in her serious, hoarse little voice, " a great ship was sailing along at night. . . . "

And then, steadily, unfalteringly, line by line, word by word, quaintly reproducing every inflexion of her mother's voice, Molly told Denis Cradock the tale of the man who died to save a little girl in a white frock.

" He could save others, but not himself ! " she concluded, sinking back on to her heels and folding her hands again, to indicate that the story was ended. " Now you know why I envy you. I hope it wasn't too long a story. Are you tired ? " She looked up anxiously.

Cradock did not reply. His thoughts were far away—following his wife, *splendide mendax* for his unworthy sake, through all those years of neglect. Presently he emerged from his reverie.

" And you had this story from your mother ? " he asked, in a low voice.

" Yes."

" Has she told it to you often ? "

" Over and over again. Joan calls it ' The Legend.' It never varies. Denny once asked Mother how she knew it so well, and she said she thought it must be written on her heart. Denny was quite little then : of course he doesn't ask questions like that now. He and Joan aren't impulsive any more—at least, Joan isn't. I know they feel just as I do, though."

" It would be rather splendid," continued Cradock unsteadily, " to have children who remembered you as that sort of man."

Far away a church clock chimed. Molly scrambled to her feet, shook herself, and hitched up the pink silk stockings of ceremony —her most cherished articles of attire—which she had donned in honour of the guest.

" I suppose I ought to go in now," she said. " It must be late. I'll tell Mother I told you The Legend ; I know she won't mind your knowing. Perhaps you would like to hear it from her yourself. Ask her to-morrow, at lunch."

" I'm not quite sure," replied Cradock, stepping out of the punt and holding it steady, " that I shall be at lunch to-morrow."

" Oh—why ? " There was genuine consternation in Molly's voice.

" I may have to go away—rather unexpectedly. Will you tell your mother ? I've had some news."

" Not bad news ? "

" No, not bad news : only—sudden. I think I'll say good night now."

Molly hurriedly snatched up the autograph book.

" Will you sign this, please ? " she asked.

" Of course I will."

" There's enough light under that big Chinese lantern, I think." She handed him the volume, with its inseparable companion, the fountain pen. " Will you be away long, do you think ? "

" I don't know," said Cradock, writing. " I'm not sure. I may have to go abroad again." He handed back the book. " There you are, Molly."

" Thanks most awfully," said Molly ecstatically. " I'll lay it down here for a minute, for the ink to dry. We shall miss you, Captain Conway."

" Will you ? "

" Yes—all of us."

" And I shall miss you. You. Molly, more than any of them."

" Don't ! " said Molly, with entire sincerity. " I'm an awful little idiot, really. I'm impulsive, and sentimental, and an Ancestor Worshipper——"

Suddenly Cradock blazed out :

" Go on being impulsive, Molly ! Go on with your Ancestor Worship ! For all you know, you may be doing some poor old ancestor a lot of good keeping him on a pedestal—even though he may not be entitled to it ! "

" All right, I will." Molly offered a hand. " Good night ! "

Cradock took the hand, and held it.

" Molly," he said, " I have a daughter about your age. Will you give me a kiss for her ? "

" Certainly," replied Molly, with great cordiality—" if you don't mind my telling Mother. She once told me I could do anything of that kind I liked, so long as I told her directly afterwards."

Cradock laughed.

" I accept your terms. Tell your mother. I don't think she'll be angry."

Molly, standing on tiptoe, reached up and kissed her hero reverently upon the cheek. Suddenly a pair of strong arms closed round her, and for the first time in her life she felt herself crushed to a man's heart. But the man did not hurt her, or frighten her. He kissed her with infinate tenderness on the forehead and on the eyes ; and then released her.

" Good-bye, Molly ! " he said gently.

" Good-bye ! "

Molly ran up the path towards the house, turning, after the pretty fashion of the young, to wave her hand before finally disappearing.

Denis Cradock stood gazing after the last flutter of her pink skirts ; then he turned away, rather heavily, and stepped down into the punt. A footstep sounded upon the planking of the landing-stage behind him : his wife was standing a few feet away.

" Hallo, Mildred ! " he said.

" What have you been saying to her ? " she demanded fiercely. " What have you been telling her ? "

" Oddly enough, very little." He was his cool self again, almost. " She has told me a good deal, though." He picked up his punt-pole. " I gave her a message for you : I expect she'll deliver it when she sees you. I must go now." He slid the end of the pole into the water and turned his back.

" Denis ! "

" Yes ? "

" What have you been saying to that defence-less child ? "

He turned and shook his head gravely.

" Milly, Molly may be a child, but she is not defenceless. She wears the most effective armour in the world."

" I don't understand."

" You will, presently. Good night ! " He set his weight to the pole, then checked himself. " Milly," he asked, " may I say something ? "

" What is it ? "

" Only this. If I had a hat on—I would take it off to you ! "

With a thrust of the pole he set his barque gliding towards the mouth of the backwater. Then he paused and looked back at her—an upright, youthful, engaging figure of a man— with a smile on his lips.

" Good night, Milly ! " he said again.

" Good night—Denny ! "

Next moment he was gone.

" DID you enjoy yourself—Phyllis ? "

" Rather—Denny ! "

Half an hour works wonders when we are twenty-one ; and, to be frank, Denny and Phyllis had wasted no time over the fireworks. Having moored their canoe beneath a friendly willow half-way up the reach, they were devoting the balance of their evening to the furtherance of their mutual acquaintance, with the progress indicated above.

Denny continued :

" Have one more cigarette, just to please me ? "

" All right ! "

Denny leaned forward and held the match for Phyllis ; Phyllis held the hand that held the match, to steady it. The moon was shining too.

Suddenly the heavens were illuminated by a final fiery eruption and a distant band began to play " God Save the King ! " The pair in the canoe sighed.

" That means home for us," said Denny. He sat up reluctantly. " I say, will you let me take you out again to-morrow, and I'll teach you to punt?"

"Isn't it very difficult?"

"You'll learn all right, with plenty of practice. In a fortnight I'll undertake to make quite a good performer of you; and in a month, or six weeks——"

"But I can't stay here for ever."

"You must!"

Miss Harding's dark eyes, gazing bashfully riverward, fell upon a passing craft proceeding up stream under the propulsion of a single practised hand.

"How well that man punts," she observed, *à propos des bottes*.

"It's Conway," said Denny. "He'll have an awkward time getting home, with all that pack of launches and punts coming down— and this current. They're a hopeless lot, too. Trippers, most of them, with no more idea of how to sit a boat than—I say, look at that!"

Two pleasure boats, packed to the gunwales with humorous young men and appreciative young women, were sweeping down stream with oars interlocked, the occupants of one vessel engaged in a playful attempt to capsize the other.

"Perishing asses!" growled Denny. "Just above the weir, too! My God, look!"

A third craft—a punt containing two women

and a little girl in a white frock, the latter
crawling precariously about on the forward locker
—had suddenly swung athwart the stream, right
in the track of the oncoming and unheeding com-
batants. Before anyone had time to realise what
was happening, there was a rending crash, and
the punt, struck fair amidships, heeled half over.

Shrieks   followed—confusion—then   naked
panic ; for, although the punt had righted
itself, it was seen that the little girl had been
thrown overboard by the shock of the collision
and was now drifting rapidly down stream
several yards ahead of the pursuing flotilla—
and gaining. Her white frock, spread upon
the water and evidently buoying her up for the
moment, was plainly visible in the moonlight.

" Come on ! " shouted Denny, pushing aside
the branches of the willow and getting madly
to work with his paddle. " Let's try to cut
her off ! She'll pass here in a couple of minutes.
If she gets over to the far side of Abbot's Island,
the weir——"

Phyllis pointed excitedly across the river.

" Look, look ! " she cried. " He's seen her ! "

The man in the racing-punt, who a moment
before had been poling his way up stream with
easy deliberation, had suddenly changed his
course. His light craft was now racing
diagonally across the current, making con-

siderable leeway, but progressing nevertheless. Barely a hundred yards below him lay the sharp point of Abbot's Island, buttressed with stakes and wattles, and splitting the river like a wedge. On the near side ran the comparatively placid channel leading to the lock; beyond, the current slid swiftly towards the sluice-gates above the weir.

" He'll have to hurry," panted Denny, " or she'll get into the eddy above the point of the island. . . . It's all right : he's going to do it ! "

The flying punt was within a few yards of the glimmering bundle on the water. The man dropped his pole, and ran forward. Straightway his unwieldy craft, released from control, slewed broadside on to the current, and lost way. A cry went up from the boats.

" He's missed her ! " gasped Denny . . . . No—I say, look ! Oh, well done ! Did you see that ? Come on, let's get him ! "

There came a roar from the pursuing flotilla, for Denny Cradock's father, having missed his target by inches had taken a header, without hesitation, into the swirling waters of the river. A moment later he came to the surface again, with the child in his arms.

Another roar went up, and a motor-launch shouldered its way out of the ruck and went flying in pursuit. Denny's canoe was a good second.

MILDRED found her younger daughter consuming biscuits and lemonade in the drawing-room, thrilled to the soul by her romantic evening and fairly bubbling with confidences.

The marvellous voyage was described in detail.

"And what did you and Captain Conway talk about, dear?" she asked.

"Oh, quite a lot of things. He's had an awfully interesting life, but rather a sad one, I'm afraid. By the way, he gave me a message for you, Mother."

"What is it, dear?"

"He's very sorry, but he can't come to lunch to-morrow. He has to go to London. Isn't it a shame. He said he might even be going abroad."

"Alone?" asked Mildred quickly.

"I don't know: he didn't say. He's had some news, though."

"From—where?"

"I'm not sure. But it wasn't bad news. I asked him that particularly."

"Just sudden?" suggested Mildred.

" That's exactly what he said."

Mildred gazed at her daughter's flushed and eager face, pondering certain matters in her heart. She felt unaccountably at peace. Something very unexpected and momentous had occurred in her relations with her husband—and instinct told her that Molly held the key.

" Come into the garden, dear," she said. " It's cooler there—and darker."

Molly slipped her arm confidingly into her mother's, and they strolled out upon the lawn.

" You haven't told me, Littlest," said Mildred presently, " what sort of things you and Captain Conway talked about."

" I did most of the talking, I think," replied Molly apologetically. " But he told me some things about his early life, and his friendship with Father. He seemd to know him very well. Then I told him the Legend." Molly, conscious that her mother's arm had stiffened within her own, looked up. " There was no harm in telling him, was there ? "

" What did he say when you told him ? "

Molly considered.

" He said nothing for a while," she replied. " Then he said he thought it must be rather a splendid thing for a man to be remembered by his children in that way. I think that was all.

After that he said he must go, and we said
good night. . . . I say, Mother ? "

" Yes, dear."

" I kissed him when we said good night. I
told him first about telling you, and he said
he didn't think you'd be angry. Are you ? "

" No, dear, I'm not angry."

" He has a daughter about my age. Did you
know ? "

" Yes, dear, I knew. Hark ! What's that ? "
Confused sounds were audible upon the river.

" I expect it's the end of the fireworks,"
said Molly, running ahead; " but I'll go and see."

Mildred stopped short, trembling violently.

" Molly, don't go ! " she cried suddenly.
" Come back, dear ! "

Molly obediently retraced her footsteps.

" All right, Mother," she said. " Why, what's
the matter ? You're all cold and shaky. Take
my arm. Lean on me—hard ! "

" I'm all right, dear ; I'm feeling a little
chilly, that's all. Run and get me a wrap,
will you ? "

Molly raced away, intent upon first aid. The
moment she was gone Mildred thrust her way
through the laurels, and ran to the towpath,
emerging exactly opposite the end of Abbot's
Island—just in time to see a miracle happen,
and a lie nearly sixteen years old come true.

WITH heavy feet Sir Anthony entered the pleasantly lit drawing-room. It was almost midnight. Mildred was sitting on the sofa, very still, with Molly's hand in hers. At a sign from the old man, the little girl rose and tiptoed from the room.

Mildred looked up. She was very pale, but entirely composed.

" They have found him ? " her lips asked.

" Yes—by the stakes above the weir."

" He was—dead ? "

" Yes. He appears to have gone under the moment they took the child from his arms. He held her up—she was more frightened than hurt— and cried out, ' Here she is ! ' Then, without any warning at all, he slipped back and was gone. He must have been more exhausted than he looked. He didn't seem to try to save himself, Denny said ; but they saw his face and he was smiling. He was a brave fellow." The old gentleman's voice shook. "They are bringing him here: it is the nearest place."

" It is the only place," said Mildred.

Then she sat silent again, with folded hands, thinking her own thoughts—and who are we to attempt to penetrate them ? Gradually her expression changed ; the hard lines began to disappear from about her mouth. The hunted look in her eyes was gone ; in its place the tender gaze which her husband had detected there, for a brief moment, that very afternoon, had come back. This time one felt it had come back for good.

Once she spoke.

" I suppose we shall never know," she said half to herself.

It was Sir Anthony who broke the silence.

" He was a fortunate man at the last," he said soberly. " Most of us would like to die at the biggest moment of our lives. Death under such circumstances puts Paid to any account."

Mildred looked up.

" Uncle Tony, do you know with whom he spent the last hour of his life ? "

" Molly, wasn't it ? "

" Yes, it was Molly. And it was Molly who found the way out for us."

" Molly ? " said the old man in surprise. " The Littlest of the Hostages ? "

" Yes. In all simplicity, in all innocence, she found the way out for us—and for him."

Sir Anthony laid his hand upon Mildred's.

" I was right ? " he asked.

Mildred nodded.

" Yes. The white spot you spoke of—it was

there, all the time ! And without knowing it, Molly revealed it. When he left her to-night he had accepted her standard—her estimate of himself. He was going away—for good."

The old man bowed his head.

" The miracle," he said softly—" the miracle ! But how do you know this ? "

" From what Molly told me. And—from what he said to me himself."

" You saw him, then ? "

" Yes. He was standing in his punt, just leaving. He looked so tall, and vigorous, and young, in that light ! "

" What did he say ? "

" Very little ; and what he said was spoken in his old, careless, flippant fashion. But it told me all I wanted to know, and—it repaid me for much. . . After that, we said good-night to one another, and he went away. I shall always be glad we—said good-night to one another." She covered her face.

" You loved him, Mildred ? "

" Always ! "

Sir Anthony rose gently to his feet, and left her.

*   *   *   *   *

Out in the garden, flitting across the lawn like a forlorn little ghost, he found Molly, obviously anxious for company.

" I've been down to the backwater," she explained. " I left my autograph-book there.

It was pretty dark ; the lanterns have all gone out. Where's Mother ? "

" In there, resting for a moment."

" Captain Conway was a very old friend of hers," continued the little girl confidentially ; " and he died just the way my father died. That's what upset Mother : it has brought things back. It must be rather splendid to have known two men who could die like that."

" I dare say your mother is well content, my dear, in having known one," said the old man. " Ah, here she is ! "

Mildred was standing in the veranda behind them, with a look of infinite peace on her face.

" Time for bed, Littlest ! " she said, with all her old authoritative smile.

" I just ran down to the backwater for my autograph-book, Mother. Molly displayed the precious volume. " Almost the last thing he did was to sign it for me. He has only put his initials, though : there they are—' D. C.' "

" The same initials as Denny," said Sir Anthony thoughtfully.

" So they are. I never noticed. And he's written them on Lord Roberts' private page. Of course he didn't know. But I'm glad now : aren't you, Mother ? "

" Yes, dear. Glad and proud—now."

THE END

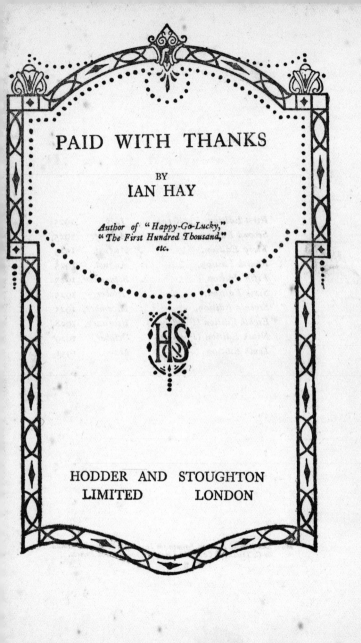

PAID WITH THANKS

BY

IAN HAY

Author of "Happy-Go-Lucky,"
"The First Hundred Thousand,"
etc.

HODDER AND STOUGHTON
LIMITED   LONDON

First Edition, Published	.	July,	1925
Second Edition, ,,	.	August,	1925
Third Edition, ,,	.	August,	1925
Fourth Edition, ,,	.	August,	1925
Fifth Edition, ,,	.	September,	1925
Sixth Edition, ,,	.	October,	1925
Seventh Edition, ,,	.	December,	1925
Eighth Edition (F'cap 8vo.)	.	February,	1928
Ninth Edition (Popular)	.	October,	1929
Tenth Edition ,,	.	May,	1931

Made and Printed in Great Britain for Hodder & Stoughton, Limited by C. Tinling & Co., Ltd., Liverpool, London and Prescot.

Contents

The second half of this story was originally presented in dramatic form by Mr. Robert Loraine, at the St. James's Theatre, under the title of " The Happy Ending."